THE GANG
OF
SEVEN

· A POST WORLD WAR II NOVEL ·

PETER HAASE

Outskirts Press, Inc.
Denver, Colorado

The Gang of Seven
A Post World Ward II Novel
All Rights Reserved
Copyright © 2007 Peter Haase
V 3.0

Cover Image © 2007 JupiterImages Corporation
All Rights Reserved. Used With Permission.

Outskirts Press
http://www.outskirtspress.com

ISBN-13: 978-1-4327-0793-4

Outskirts Press and the "OP" logo are trademarks belonging to
Outskirts Press, Inc.

Printed in the United States of America

CONTENTS

Heinz burst through the door and with him came a swirl of snow flurries. Chill air followed him into the single-room bungalow.

"What the hell happened to you?" Karl demanded. "You were supposed to be here an hour ago. Where the hell were you?" Karl was the oldest among them and they respected him. They had not elected him to be their leader; he was a natural.

Heinz was only sixteen, innocent looking, blond and pale, but smart. "Couldn't get away. MPs checked the place out. I pretended I worked there. Then they stood around on the loading platform until their truck came. I had to look busy until they left."

"So, how many did you get?"

"Twenty-two. They're under the tarp at the rear door in the storage shed."

"The storage shed?" The one they called Kurzer shouted in mock amusement. "How are we gonna get them out of there?"

"Yeah, I'm not breaking the lock," Manfred chimed in. "I fix locks, I don't break'em."

Karl silenced them with a hand gesture. "Krista," he said to the girl lying on the old, tattered couch, with her head in his lap. "Krista, you'll have to make friends with that woman in charge there. Can you do that?"

She had been sleeping or dozing. "What? Who? Friends with who?" She lifted her head, pushed a strand of dirty-blonde hair from her face.

Heinz removed a big, four-inch long key from his coat pocket. "No problem. Key always hangs on a nail inside the door." He put the key back in his pocket. "Frau Lange... she's okay. She thinks of me as the son she never had. She wrote the slip out for 148 cans. Even she doesn't know they only got 126."

Krista went back to sleep, unconcerned with what the guys were talking about.

"Is that safe?" asked Klaus interrupting his card game with Hans-Peter. They sat on folding chairs, an upturned barrel between them. "I mean, who is that woman?"

"She does the inventory. Worked there all through the war. She's okay. Is friends with my mom ever since we moved here to Schlutup."

"So, how're we gonna do it?" Manfred, a locksmith apprentice before he was drafted into the military, had yet to overcome his reluctance to break with his "professional ethics", as he called it.

Heinz explained. "The door is always locked from the outside. So, when someone leaves through the backdoor, he needs to take the key with him if he wants to get back in. Simple as that."

"Oh, I get it. It's not really a break-in, then. With the key—it's almost legit." Manfred feigned a sigh of relief.

Karl was not completely convinced. "Friends with your mom, huh? Heinz, how well do you know this woman? She's not gonna snitch on us, is she?"

"Look, Karl, we've done this before. She's beyond suspicion. She works there for like ten years."

"Are you kidding? We've never done this before. You got us one or two cans, we sold'em on the black market. But twenty-two...?"

"They won't find out they're missing until tomorrow when they unload the truck at the army depot—if they even count them at all."

"All right. Let's hope so. It's all clear then. Here's the plan. Half an hour after the last shift, that's at nine-thirty, Heinz, you go ahead with the key. I follow with Klaus, Hans-Peter and Schwarzer. Manfred and Kurzer stay behind with the cart, wait at the boathouse. The MPs come around to check at midnight and then again by three in the morning. At six the first shift comes in. Should be easy enough for us. We have over two hours. Now, what about if there's snow?"

"It's gonna turn to rain later," one of them said.

"May I make a suggestion?" Manfred asked in his semi-refined manner of speaking. "If there's snow, you all walk away in different directions so they don't know what track to follow."

"Carrying the heavy cans? They weigh four and a half kilos each, that's ten pounds. Some of us will have to carry four of them."

"Calm down, guys." Karl took control. "We carry the cans straight down to the boathouse and load 'em onto the cart. And if there's snow or slush on the ground, we go back and mess up our tracks. Kurzer, you go with Manfred, okay? Help him with the cart. Is that clear?"

There was some mumbling but they knew that was the way it had to be.

"We need some kind of bags or something, you know, something to carry the stuff." Klaus was thinking aloud.

"I mean, how do we handle three or four cans?"

"Good question. Schwarzer, you said the other day something about burlap sacks in the basement of that produce shop over at Falkenstrasse. Like potato sacks."

"I'll see if they're still there. I can be back in an hour. What time is it?"

"Quarter past eight." Manfred was the only one who had a watch.

"I'll be back in less than an hour," said Schwarzer. "Klaus, come with me?"

They both left. It was still snowing. The snow gave a luminescent transparency to the otherwise dark night. Dim lights came through curtained windows of the adjacent dwellings in this former garden colony. Since the destruction of half the town in the bomb raid of 1942, families had made the bungalows and sheds on the outskirts of Schlutup their permanent homes.

Hans-Peter put the deck of cards back into their case and stretched his legs, leaning back in his chair. Karl stroked Krista's

hair as she cuddled close to him for warmth. The others sat on mat-
tresses piled up on one side of the room. They had a wood fire going in the stove, but the walls lacked insulation and the icy wind
seemed to blow right through them.

The kettle on the stove whistled thinly as the water began to
boil. Schwarzer had put the kettle on to make tea before he and
Klaus left to look for the burlap sacks.

Kurzer got up. "Who wants tea?"

"Forget the tea; pour some of that disgusting booze in the water, and some sugar," Manfred grumbled. "And put another log on
that fire. Please. It's freezing in here."

"No alcohol," Karl said with authority. "Until afterwards."

Schwarzer and Klaus came back a few minutes past nine. Each
had a bundle of old potato sacks. "Piece o' cake." Klaus threw his
bundle on the floor.

"Yeah," Schwarzer added. "The broken cellar window wasn't
fixed yet, so we got in easy."

"Nobody saw you?" asked Karl.

"Nope. Too cold out there. Nobody roaming around. Got something to warm us up?" Klaus headed for the cupboard to pick up a
mug.

"How about some of that *Aquavit*?"

"Not until we get back here. Have some hot water and brown
sugar, or tea."

"Oh, come on, Karl. We're freezing."

"Stand by the fire. No booze until later."

***

Hans-Peter and Kurzer stood behind the boathouse, sheltered from
the wind. The snow turned to freezing rain. Kurzer wore a peacoat
from the *Kriegsmarine*, the German Navy, a watch cap and woolen
gloves; still he shivered in the cold wet night. Hans-Peter, in a
converted army greatcoat, stomped his feet trying to keep warm.
They had brought the two-wheeled pushcart they used to carry
firewood from the nearby forest back to the house.

While they waited, the others, except Krista, made their way to the storage building of the fish packing plant. This once lucrative cannery was located near the harbor where the only two trawlers still in operation had their berths.

The floodlight illuminating the yard between the factory and the storehouse left the rear entrance in the dark. Heinz unlocked the backdoor. They entered silently and removed the tarp. Just enough light came from the yard through a high window to reveal the neatly stacked commercial-sized cans, labeled **Baltic Herring in Brine. Military Rations. Civilian Consumption prohibited**.

Karl stuffed four cans in his burlap sack and hefted them onto his shoulder. The others followed suit. Heinz, being the youngest and the smallest of the gang, took three. Between the five of them, they carried away nineteen cans. Bent under their weight, they hurried through the slush and reached the boathouse at the water's edge. Hans-Peter and Kurzer loaded the goods into the cart.

"Did you leave any tracks?" Hans-Peter asked.

"It's all turning to slush already. I have to go back anyway, hang the key back on the nail," said Heinz.

"You didn't leave the key? You dumb ox."

"Look, there are three more cans. We don't want to leave those. Kurzer, come with me. We take care of the tracks if there are any, hang up the key and pick up the last three cans."

"Hurry up, then. We're not sticking around," Karl cautioned them. "The cart's overloaded as it is. And don't get caught."

Heinz and Kurzer went back to the warehouse.

Two of the guys pushed the heavy cart that groaned under the weight. The others walked behind. They arrived at their cottage well before midnight. Heinz and Kurzer came in shortly after them and put down their three cans. Then they all went out to unload the cart and stacked the cans in the corner behind a partition.

"How did it go?" asked Krista who had stayed behind, tending the fire in the stove. "You must be half frozen."

"Okay. It worked like clockwork. Now let's get some of that grog. Hot water, a healthy shot of that *Schnaps* and sugar." Manfred couldn't wait to let that stuff run down his throat to warm him. "Man, it is nasty out there. My feet are wet and numb."

Karl said, "all right, you guys. Two shots for each of you. I don't want anyone getting drunk or sick or something." He mumbled, "I don't know how you can drink that evil stuff anyway." Karl did not like alcohol and rarely drank. He and Krista settled on the worn couch that had once been a pretty decent piece of furniture.

Karl, twenty-six years old, was from a middle-class family in the small town of Schlutup at the Baltic Sea coast. He had been lucky during the war, although drafted into the infantry right at the start in '39. First in Poland and then in France, his supply unit always remained a few kilometers behind front lines. Later he enjoyed the good life in occupied Denmark. In August of '45 he returned to his hometown in the British occupation zone. His father had died and his mother ran off with some guy. Karl didn't stick around. He went back to Denmark, from where he shipped the rich canned Danish butter to his black market connections back home.

In the winter of 1946/47 he returned to Schlutup, the quaint North German fishing town, close to the border with the Russian zone. He met up with Manfred, Hans-Peter and Klaus who had escaped together from a Russian POW camp in the Soviet occupied zone. They made the abandoned garden shack their home.

Hans-Peter and Manfred, both nineteen years old, were taken prisoners the last weeks of the fighting. Klaus, seventeen, had been in the *Volkssturm*, the last of Hitler's contingency to try to stem the onslaught in Berlin.

Kurzer, so called because of his short and stocky build, was on his home turf. Much younger than Karl, they never met as kids on the playground or in school. His mother was killed in a bomb raid and his father was missing on the Eastern front. Drifting aimlessly, he stole potatoes, carrots, turnips or a lettuce, which he sold for cigarettes or ration coupons. Eventually he joined Karl and his friends in the garden colony where he used to harvest "his" produce in nightly escapades.

Heinz had come to Schlutup during the war from the Rhineland. His father, an engineer, had been transferred to the nearby airplane parts factory, the *Hansawerke AG*. Living in the housing complex adjacent to the *Hansawerke*, his mother found a job as supervisor at the fish packing plant. She became friends with Frau Lange who sometimes gave her a can of sardines, a mackerel or a herring. At the end of the war the cannery was shut down and did not reopen until a year later. Heinz's mother lost her job, but the family did not return to their home near Cologne. Heinz still lived with his parents, but he spent most of his time with the Gang in the Garden colony.

Then there was Schwarzer, an odd fellow in his early twenties. Of dark complexion and coal-black hair, he looked like a Gypsy. Originally from Silesia, nobody knew much about him, nor how he happened to become one of the Gang of Seven, as they referred to themselves. Quiet and amiable, Schwarzer always helped where help was wanted, never complained, never offended anyone.

Krista was tolerated and respected by the Gang as Karl's girlfriend. Nobody questioned her presence at the house. Karl had brought her across the border when he returned from one of his trips into the Russian zone. She had been raped repeatedly when the Soviets occupied her town. A lieutenant of the Red Army rescued her and she became his mistress. He turned violent when drunk, and that happened often. How Karl found her and managed to bring her back with him remained unexplained.

After the return from their successful expedition to the cannery, they emptied a bottle of that potato *Schnaps*, marked *Feiner Aquavit, 38% Vol.* Alcohol, banned in the Western occupation zones, was available only as contraband smuggled across the border from the Soviet zone.

Karl had brought back a couple of bottles from 'over there' when he visited an army buddy of his. "There's money in it," his friend had told him. "I can get all the *Schnaps* you want and you bring me clothing, cigarettes, canned meat or fish—anything you get your hand on."

***

"Did you see Frau Lange? We have nothing today. I don't know what to give your father when he comes home from the lumberyard. The watery broth from Timm's Butchery has hardly any fat floating on top."

Heinz had come home at noon after the night of the break-in. "She couldn't give me anything. The trawlers couldn't go out due to the weather." His mother would have been horrified if he told her of the break-in at the plant the night before.

Hungry, with a foul taste in his mouth from the booze and the raw sugar, he asked her, "Mom, isn't there any of that barley bread left?"

"You can't eat that. It's hard as a rock. It'll break your teeth."

"I can dunk it in the broth, if you heat it up for me. At least it must have some flavor from the sausages they cooked in it."

"The gas didn't come on this morning. I can't heat the water. Will you help me light the stove?" She sighed. The heat in the building had not been turned on all winter. "When your father comes home, you have to go and get firewood. We're almost out."

To find dry twigs and branches, they had to go deeper and deeper into the forest, right up to the border. People had started to cut down trees, which was strictly forbidden.

"We can go to jail for that, you know. It's becoming more dangerous every day."

"But what are we to do? What are people to do? How can we live?" She implored him. "When will this end?"

"Mom, I'm tired. I'll get the fire going, then I want to sleep for an hour. Later I'll go get wood with Dad."

"I don't want you to hang out with that gang, Heinz. What are you doing, anyway?"

"Nothing. I'll get us some food, or stamps. I'll figure something out."

He used the last of the kindling to light the fire and his mother put on some of the watery broth she was able to get at Timm's. Then they both dunked stale chunks of bread into the hot briny liquid and ate it; it barely tasted of meat, but there was a hint of bay leaves, cumin or some such spice. Still hungry, Heinz went into the bedroom. He slept until his father came home. They borrowed their neighbor's wagon and, with the fading daylight, went into the woods.

"How much longer you have to work at that place, Dad?"

"They convicted me to six weeks labor, but I got that certificate from the doctor. He found I had an ulcer. I'll report in tomorrow and go on sick leave. I don't know what I'll do then."

"You have an ulcer?"

"Naw. Not yet, anyway. That doctor... He's okay."

Heinz's father had been a member of the Nazi Party to keep his job as an engineer. Now he was being punished for it in the so-called *Entnazifizierungs* process. He never was a sympathizer, hated the whole bunch of them—Hitler, Himmler, Göring, Göbbels and the generals, too. But he was an engineer; what could he do?

"Want to cut down a tree, Dad, and be done with it? It's dark enough. Nobody will see us. I don't think we can find any dry wood or dead branches."

"Let's get a little deeper into the woods." Then they stopped. "Here, this one will do. Looks like a young beech. I hope the saw is still sharp enough."

They worked hard with their inadequate tools to cut the little tree down and then saw the trunk and the branches into three-foot pieces. They went home pulling the old wagon, with the bigger chunks on the bottom, the branches on top.

"What you got there, hm?" Their neighbor, a quarrelsome old man, spotted them as they reached the apartment house. "Looks like fresh wood to me. You wouldn't cut down a tree now, would you?"

"Hey, neighbor, you know how it is. Tree was down already. We just cut it up."

"I'll take half of the wood, if you know what I mean. You don't want any trouble, right? Let's say, it's for lending you the cart and I keep my mouth shut. Got my drift?"

The winter of 1946/47 was tough. Malnourished, in unheated homes, threadbare clothes and inadequate footwear, old people suffered the most. The stores were empty; what bread, meat and produce there was, was of the poorest quality. Rations were below the minimum needed for survival. Those with no access to the black market to supplement their rations, died of starvation. "Even the last year of the war was better than this," people complained. Of course, that was not counting the fear of air raids or the Gestapo.

The Gang of Seven had what it takes to survive. They were organized and disciplined under Karl's guidance, but most of all they were determined and fearless.

Schwarzer came back from an excursion into town. "Karl, can I speak to you for a moment?" In his unassuming manner he steered Karl away from the others and continued in a low voice. "I don't know if it's any good, but at the freight terminal, on the outer siding, there's a rail car loaded with cooking oil."

"Yeah? What about it?"

"Some people could do a lot of cooking with a carload of oil, is all I am saying."

Klaus came over to them. "The oil? Yeah, I know. Can't be done, though. MPs swarming all over the place."

"What do you know about it?"

"I know this girl at the terminal office. Gudrun's her name. She works there, sees all the freight papers and stuff. That cargo goes to Hamburg for shipment to England."

Hans-Peter heard them talking. "Why can't it be done? If it can't be done, I am your man. That's my specialty, jobs that can't be done."

Then Manfred also joined them. "What are you talking about? A freight car? Now with that I have no trouble. Somebody's home—that would give me some cause for, eh... consideration. I might find it, let's say... unethical." He always expressed himself in that half-educated manner. "You know, a locksmith has to be mindful of his reputation."

"Yeah, hold it a minute. We'll get back to your reputation. Let's see what we have here." Karl thought for a moment, then he called, "Heinz, get over here."

They decided to send Heinz, innocent looking and the youngest of the Gang, to take a look at the railroad car, how the doors are locked and where the guards are. Then Karl turned back to Klaus. "Find out from that girl what's in the car and when it's leaving for Hamburg. You know how to do that? Is she in love with you?"

Klaus blushed. "How do I know? I only walked her home the other day and we talked."

"Yeah well, talk some more. But real casual-like. Don't tell her anything. Don't tell her about the Gang of Seven."

Heinz strolled along the siding. Indeed, there were MPs inside the terminal and others outside checking a freight train that had just arrived. Hidden by a locomotive belching white steam, Heinz had a chance to get close to the single car on the far side.

Hans-Peter and Manfred stood talking in front of the terminal building, while Klaus went inside to see Gudrun. It was midday, and she would soon go on her lunch break.

"I want to know what this girl looks like. Klaus is shy," said Hans-Peter. "I'd get real cozy with her until she tells me all she knows about the car and what's in it."

"Here they come," said Manfred. The girl came out, wearing a black coat, woolen hat and boots. Klaus followed her. Together they crossed the cobblestone plaza and went into one of the side streets.

Yep, I'd do her in a minute. And she'd enjoy it too, Hans-Peter dreamed.

Heinz made a wide turn around the station and then casually joined Hans-Peter and Manfred.

"Big padlock on the sliding door. There is this lever that hooks into…"

"Yeah, I know what it looks like," Manfred, the professional, cut him off. "How big is the padlock, in your estimation?"

"I climbed up on the running board and checked it out good. It's bigger than my hand and weighs at least a kilo. Real heavy duty, that thing. Has a flap over the keyhole."

"Should be easy for you." Hans-Peter was more concerned with what comes after the lock has been opened or broken. "The door. Now, that's the problem. Will it slide?"

"All right, I see no obstacle in the lock. The door—that will be our main concern. Let's go and apprise Karl of our findings. He and Kurzer have a personal intimate knowledge of the town. They have to work out our route of escape."

Hans-Peter said, "We have to figure out how to divert attention. Set a fire or something." Then he thought about the girl. *If Klaus won't, I will.*

Kurzer had been on a mission that morning. He had taken one of the ten-pound herring cans and exchanged it for a large chunk of horsemeat. From time to time farmhands at the Selmhof a few kilometers outside of town slaughtered a horse. They distributed the meat among their friends and the town's people who traded valuable objects, rugs and silverware, and china, paintings and jewelry for farm products.

For hours a stew with vegetables and potatoes was simmering on the stove, filling the room with fragrant aromas of herbs and spices. Kurzer always was their man when it came to provisioning.

"So, that's the situation. We have only a few hours." The meal over, they sat around and tried to come up with a plan. Karl asked Klaus again, "Are you sure they hook that car up to the train tomorrow?"

"Karl, all I know is what she told me. But she should know, she sees all the schedules and stuff. It's her job."

"Okay." He talked to Hans-Peter now. "Distraction, you said. A fire... What do you mean? Where? This side of the terminal building? What will burn there?"

"No. Has to be in the terminal. The building itself." Hans-Peter was not only the funniest, he was also the most ruthless among them.

"Burn down the building? Man, are you mad? For a few cans of oil?"

"You have a better suggestion? Oil usually comes in nine-kilo containers for commercial use. If that's what it is, we can each carry two of them. That's a lot of oil."

"No way. We are no arsonists. You a comedian or something?" Karl shook his head. "What about transportation? If we pull it off, how are we getting away with the loot?"

"We'll figure something out." Hans-Peter was amused, not offended by Karl's rebuff. "You're good at that. Transportation is your thing."

"That cart's no good on cobblestones. And another thing: when would we do it? At night? Maybe in the daytime. Less conspicuous with all kinds of people about. We blend in."

"Yeah, right," Kurzer chuckled. "With a couple of oil drums on our backs... Sure, we blend right in." He had been quiet until now. "Listen, we don't have to take the stuff all the way through town. I know these people at Kanalstrasse. We can get there through the lumberyard of the old sawmill. Karl, you know the place I'm talking about."

"Yeah, but who are those people?"

"The Johannsens. They are the ones who gave me the tip on Selmhof and the horsemeat. Wolfgang is a few years older than me."

"We don't need more people to know about us."

"He already knows about us. He has his own gang. They cross the border all the time. Textile mostly."

Karl turned to Heinz. "Is that where your father works? Can you go back there and find out how we get from the siding to the lumberyard? Is there a fence? Is there a guard, a night watchman, a dog?"

"I don't know the place, but, yes, that's where he worked before he got sick. Has an ulcer." Heinz hesitated. "Karl, do I have to go? I mean, I'll do it, but I really want to bring them some of that meat. For my father, you know. You said I could."

Karl, the fair and considerate leader, said, "Yeah, okay. You go ahead. Krista, give Heinz some of that stew. Give him the rest of it. We'll be all right." He shook Heinz by the shoulder. "Sorry your dad got sick."

They all nodded and Krista wrapped the pot with the leftover in newspaper.

"That's all right. He's not really that sick. Thanks, Krista. Thanks, guys." Heinz left with the gift for his parents.

"But I want you back here," Karl called after him. "We still have to figure out what to do about that oil." Karl was intrigued by the idea and the more they talked about it, the more excited he became. Leaning over toward Kurzer he said, "Will you go and check it out? Be back here, say in an hour, hour and a half. If it can be done, it has to be tonight."

Kurzer went to snoop around the freight station and then knocked at the Johannsen's door. Wolfgang's mother was alone. They went into the living room to talk. Wolfgang was not at home and his father was still at work. Herr Johannsen was employed as a tailor for the occupation troops, which gave him access to fabric, clothing, food and cigarettes. The family was doing all right.

"We'll come in through the backdoor into the basement, Frau Johannsen; you won't even hear us." Kurzer had to convince her that this was a sure thing, although he himself wasn't so sure. "You get your share of the oil, of course," he assured the woman.

"Okay," said Frau Johannsen. "A whole container of oil, you say? Sure. I'll tell my husband to leave the door unlocked, but there's no gate in the fence between our garden and the lumberyard. You'll have to climb."

Kurzer returned to the bungalow in the garden community. "There's only a hedge between the rail siding and the lumberyard. The sawmill is shut down; it's just a lumber depot and there's nobody there at night. We have to climb over a fence to get to the Johannsens'. I saw it. Two meters. By the way, I promised the woman a can of that oil."

"All right. Let's go for it." Karl laid out his plan. "We don't know the best time to make our move, so we leave here, say nine o'clock, hide in the bushes below the embankment and wait for the right moment. We should find out more about the MPs—when they check, where they are stationed—but we only have tonight. So, we'll hide and observe. As long as it takes. Is that clear?"

"Who will keep an eye on the guards while I am up on the running board working the lock?" asked Manfred. "Somebody better signal me, if they come around that side of the car."

"We'll all be there and observe what their routines are. Then we decide. Schwarzer, you'll be the lookout on the far side, okay? Any more questions?"

"Looks like we don't have to burn down the whole place," Hans-Peter joked. "That would have been great!" He seemed to have a lot of fun with his idea.

"You'll get enough action," Karl assured him.

Heinz returned in late afternoon. Concerned with lifting heavy loads, he raised a serious question. "What if the oil is in huge barrels and not in canisters? What would we do then? Or, it could be in small bottles. I mean, we don't know."

They looked at each other. No one had thought of that. "We each take one of the sacks we used the other night," Karl said after some thinking. "If it's canisters, as we believe it is, we each take two. If it's individual bottles, we put as many as we can carry in the bags. If they're packed in boxes... I don't know. We take what we can. Barrels? I don't think so." He looked from one to the other. Darkness began to seep into the room on this winter afternoon. Their faces and gestures became vague in the fading light. "Klaus, did your girlfriend say something about how the oil is packed?"

"Ah, I don't think so. Let me think. Six by six... She said something like that. Yeah, six... Six boxes—I don't know, bundles? I didn't want to ask too much. Maybe they are six pounds, or six kilos. She had the freight manifest or what she called it."

"Bundles, huh? Sounds like cans, six wrapped together," and to Hans-Peter, "don't forget your knife; you might need it to cut a rope or open boxes. Any more questions?"

"Or to kill one of the guards," Hans-Peter joked.

Then they were silent, perhaps skeptical, apprehensive.

"Shshsh, here they come." The seven guys hid below the embankment behind the bushes and watched two soldiers, wearing MP armbands, cross over the tracks. It was the second time, ten minutes apart. They came within ten feet of the hedge as they walked around the single car and then back across the tracks toward the terminal building. Their breaths were visible in the cold night air against the dim light from the station.

"Up, Manfred. Hans-Peter, help him, hand him his tools," Karl whispered. "We stay down."

They scrambled through the gap in the hedge. Manfred climbed onto the running board and examined the lock. The cold metal numbed his gloveless hands. He had brought a flashlight but decided not to turn it on.

Schwarzer, crouching behind a shrub, had the best view of the terminal. He clicked his tongue, signal that the patrol was coming around again. There was just enough time for Manfred and Hans-

Peter to slide down the embankment into the hedge. The two MPs walked past them, talking and smoking.

"Lock's a fucking son of a bitch—excuse my language," Manfred hissed. "The thing is like an ice cube. But I will get it open. Just takes a little longer in the dark."

He climbed up again. Hans-Peter helped him and returned after a couple of minutes. "He's got it open. What now?"

"Tell him to come back here."

"Okay."

They both crouched behind the hedge before the guards came around again.

"We could just whack'em." Hans-Peter whispered and made a gesture like cutting his throat. "You know, humane-like. A cold blade under the chin…"

"Shut up. Concentrate." Karl knew Hans-Peter was more talk than action. "It's your turn. Go. Try the door. Just as we said."

Both Manfred and Hans-Peter stood on the running board, pushing at the door. Schwarzer observed the two guards stop as the door screeched for just one second in the still night. It was an awful metallic screech. Hans-Peter squeezed himself through the opening into the car. Manfred slid the door shut with another awful squeak and then scrambled back into the bushes. Not far away a dog began to bark.

The soldiers turned and came back, lingered beside the car, listened, inspected the undercarriage. They seemed to find nothing amiss and went on their way. Another dog joined in the barking.

"He's in," Manfred told Karl.

They waited. The MP patrol came around at regular intervals, stopped briefly, then continued on their round. Hans-Peter was still in the car.

Karl sent Manfred to check on the progress. "Go, see how he's doing. Maybe he can't open the door from inside."

Meanwhile, by the shine of the flashlight Hans-Peter located the stacks of aluminum canisters, roped together in bundles of six. He cut the rope of the highest bundle he could reach. Some of the cans tumbled to the floor, causing quite a racket inside the car, but outside the guys heard no more than a dull rumble. At the time the

MP guards were on the far side of the terminal; they came around again on schedule.

From then on it worked like a well-oiled machine. Hans-Peter moved canisters close to the door. As the MP patrol walked away to the far side of the terminal, Manfred went up to open the door just wide enough for two canisters to be passed through. Kurzer, Klaus, Heinz, Schwarzer and Karl came out from behind the hedge, formed a line up the embankment; each carried away two canisters. Hans-Peter helped Manfred push the door shut, then jumped down from the car and, with his two cans, followed the others.

Kurzer, one can under each arm, was the first to hurry across the yard, leading the way. As he reached the fence, Klaus caught up with him. The others followed and finally Hans-Peter joined them at the fence. Kurzer climbed the fence and received the cans on the other side. Then they all climbed over.

Just before the guards came around the corner of the car, Manfred snapped the lock into place. With no time to spare, he left his two canisters on the running board, jumped down the embankment and disappeared behind the hedge.

As he ran across the lumberyard, a shrill whistle pierced the cold winter night. Floodlights came on over the freight station and turned night into day. All the neighborhood dogs joined in the barking and howling, giving a nightly concert.

Manfred climbed the fence and was gone.

At midnight in the basement of the Johannsen's home at Kanalstrasse, the Gang of Seven found room for the twelve oil drums they had removed from the shipment destined for England.

Herr Johannsen came downstairs. "You pulled if off? How did it go? You're not gonna leave the stuff here?"

"We'll take care of it," Karl answered. "It was easier than we thought. Those guys are really stupid; they must have heard the door of that freight car open and close, and they did nothing. Almost as if they were helping us."

The canine concert of howling and barking subsided while the terminal resembled an anthill that had been disturbed. Military police swarmed all over the place, unsuccessful in their effort to locate the perpetrators.

In the morning a search party found seven potato sacks behind the hedge that separated the embankment from the lumberyard of the old sawmill.

***

In the week that followed they transported the oil containers from the Johannsen's to the garden house. One by one, on a bicycle, on foot, hidden in a bundle of clothes or in a shopping net—sometimes by night, sometimes on detours or straight through town in bright daylight—they managed to bring the precious goods undetected to their hangout.

"We have only a couple of those potato sacks left. Kurzer, can you ask your friend—what's his name, Wolfgang—how we can make knapsacks out of them? Maybe his father can get us some strips of cord or cloth?"

"Yeah, we need sewing lessons. I always wanted to be a tailor," Hans-Peter clowned. He couldn't help making some jokes about that. "Needle and thread—and while you're at it, get us a sewing machine."

"Herr Johannsen is a little difficult. You noticed that when he didn't want to keep the stuff in his basement." Kurzer was apprehensive. "I don't like the man. Always cranky, unpleasant. I'll see if Wolfgang can help us out."

The last patches of ice melted in the ditch beyond which began the former Grand Duchy of Mecklenburg. That same ditch was now the border separating the British and the Soviet occupation zones.

Beyond the ditch, on the Soviet side, was the Wesloer Moor, a wetland dangerous for the uninitiated to venture into. Standing water from the melting snow made this boggy terrain difficult to traverse even to those with local knowledge.

Karl knew the Wesloer Moor from his childhood. Before the war it had been a favorite destination for hiking and picnics. He remembered summer days with family and friends, when his mother spread mosquito repellent over his arms and legs and warned him not to stray from known paths. "There are areas where the ground is so soft, children have disappeared never to be seen again," she repeated every time. It was a spooky place. In the evenings, when the sun was low, gnarled trees and shrubs threw scary shadows across the landscape. Then they told ghost stories about lost souls lamenting and wailing in the night, attracting others to share their plight.

The Wesloer Moor was poorly patrolled by East German border police, the *VoPos*, and there were no longer any Russians in that area. Karl and Kurzer knew the path that wound its way through the desolate landscape.

Karl asked, "Schwarzer, you say two of those canisters fit in your backpack?"

"Yes, they fit side by side, only I can't close the top. But that's okay."

"Well, we need knapsacks. I mean, for those who volunteer to go. We shouldn't all go, anyway; maybe four or five of us."

They huddled together around the stove. Krista had brought home a bucket of butcher Timm's broth. A pot of potato soup simmered on the old-fashioned cast iron stove.

"Sorry, no meat. All I could add was a few carrots and a stalk of celery," she apologized. "Oh, and an onion."

"Smells good, though. Was the sausage water any good today?" asked Heinz.

"Not too bad. Actually had a few specks of fat floatin' on top."

They ladled the soup into their bowls and as they ate, the warmth spread through their bodies. One by one, they shed coats, gloves and scarves. Karl put another piece of wood on the fire. The supply had shrunk to the last couple of logs.

At the end of the war, and in the first winter afterwards, it was easy to find wood in the rubble of destroyed houses, but by 1947 all that would burn had been consumed. People were desperately waiting for an early spring and the warming rays of the sun.

"Whose turn is it to get fire wood?" Karl knew Schwarzer and Kurzer had that duty this week, but he never ordered anyone for the job nobody liked.

"Kurzer and I will go," answered Schwarzer. "As soon as it gets dark."

They advanced through the trees almost to the ditch. "That's the Wesloer Moor over there," Kurzer pointed out. He knew the moorland as well as Karl; both grew up in Schlutup. "About a hundred meters farther that way is a place where you can ford the trench. It's wide enough for carts to go across. Now there's a roadblock, but you can walk around that."

"There are no Russians? No *VoPos*?"

"Karl says, he never saw any, and he went across several times."

"So, is that where we're gonna go? It all seems too easy to me."

"It really is. They don't expect anyone to cross the moor. Farther south, in the heather, there's plenty of activity." Kurzer blew into his hands to dispel the cold. "Let's get this over with."

They had left the pushcart where the woods became too dense and walked a short distance deeper into the thicket. A pile of wood was hidden beneath some branches.

"Must have been left there by someone chased away by the forest patrol, perhaps for later recovery." They picked it up and carried it back to where they had left the cart.

"Yeah, but now it's ours. Their loss, our gain," Kurzer said happily.

With their easy find loaded into the cart they quickly were on their way home.

The weather improved and an early spring hastened their plans to turn the accumulated goods into profit. Besides the canned herring and the canisters of cooking oil, they had a supply of laundry powder, buckets of molasses and a case of strawberry jam in glass jars. All of these items were the results of previous robberies and black market transactions.

Heinz, on the urging of his parents, had joined classes at the local high school and he spent less time with the Gang.

Klaus had become more hesitant in participating in the gang's activities since the railcar incident. His girlfriend, Gudrun, found out about his involvement in the break-in.

"You and that gang of yours can get me fired," she argued. "If they find out about us, we all go to jail. You know that. I am an accomplice now."

"Okay, but they are really nice guys. I want you to meet them some day."

"Uh uh! I don't want to lose my job. If they find out..."

"All right. Don't worry."

Essentially, the Gang of Seven was reduced to five active members, not counting Krista. They discussed the border crossing.

Karl said, "We come back the same night. There is only one item we bring back: booze. It is all they have. *Schnaps*. That's it."

"But they have different kinds, right?" Manfred asked. "Or is it all the same as this *Feiner Aquavit*?" He made a face. "It really is not so *fine*."

"There is Vodka, Aquavit and *Wacholder*, a kind of gin. It's all 38% and all the same, if you ask me," said Karl, who hardly drank.

He had gone to see his buddy twice recently and they had established a rendezvous point five kilometers into the Russian zone: the barn adjacent to a farmhouse. "Walter, my buddy, he is... well he's kind of engaged to the farmer's daughter and sometimes he spends a night there."

"Does the farmer know what's going on? I mean about the furtive commerce conducted in his barn?" Manfred asked in his ridiculously stilted manner of speaking.

"And the business his daughter is conducting furtively behind his back," Hans-Peter chuckled, mimicking Manfred.

"No idea, Probably. Makes no difference," Karl said seriously. "Walter told me he has some understanding with the VoPos in the region. And," pointing to Hans-Peter, "you keep your mouth shut about Walter and this girl and stuff, okay?"

***

Lately, Karl had more than one reason for his nightly excursions into the Russian zone.

"Talking about this business with Walter," he told the Gang. In reality, talking with Walter was more likely a pretext. The exchange of the contraband items did not require a great deal of negotiations.

Kurzer was suspicious, but kept his thoughts to himself. He once asked Karl if he could come along to visit relatives of his on the other side.

"No," Karl had answered curtly, without giving an explanation.

Kurzer didn't say anything. *But,* he thought, *how long will Karl be able to conceal the real reason for his clandestine visits? Especially from Walter?*

Krista was rather naïve and unsuspecting. Neither did she care much. Karl had rescued her from that bastard Dmitre, the Russian lieutenant; Karl was her benefactor and she didn't make any demands on him.

"I have never been much of an outdoors-man," explained Manfred, the locksmith. "All this creeping across frontiers by night, getting spooked in the ghostly Wesloer Moor, is not exactly to my liking." He spoke haltingly, searching for complicated words in his limited vocabulary. "Karl, why don't you go with Schwarzer and Kurzer."

"What about me? I want to be in on the fun." Hans-Peter felt left out.

"All right, take it easy. The four of us will go, but you've got to be serious about this. It's no child's play." Karl addressed Hans-Peter specifically.

"I am always serious. Not a funny bone in my body. I've not made a joke in the last—twenty minutes." He couldn't help himself.

That evening shortly after dark they left the garden shack. Karl, Kurzer and Hans-Peter slung their makeshift knapsacks on their backs. Each of them carried two commercial-sized herring cans, not weighing more than twenty pounds, in those burlap sacks. They attached cords to them, so that they could strap them over the shoulders. Only Schwarzer had a real backpack that held two of the oil canisters.

"Don't lose your way out there. You need a flashlight?" Manfred asked. Perhaps he felt a little embarrassed for not going with them.

"No flashlight," said Karl.

"You can give that lieutenant Dmitre a kick in the ass for me," Krista called after them.

They entered upon the Wesloer Moor. "These straps are killing me," Hans-Peter complained. "They cut into my shoulders."

"Shut up," hissed Karl. "I told you to be quiet. It could just be that there's a *VoPo* around."

They walked briskly, single file, Karl leading. Schwarzer and Kurzer brought up the rear. The still air was mild in this mid-April night. Except for some soft spots, the path was dry. In less than two hours they reached the farm without incident, skirted the main house and entered the barn. Kurzer was not too surprised that Walter was not there. Instead, there was this girl. Karl did not bother to introduce her.

"Elsa, what's going on?" He gave her short, round figure a squeeze.

I thought so. That's what's going on here. They unloaded their burdens and Kurzer shot a quick glance at Hans-Peter and Schwarzer. Both lowered their eyes and turned away in a gesture meaning: oh boy, I'm staying out of this.

"The bottles are under there," said Elsa, pointing by the light of a stable lantern to a heap of straw on one side of the barn. "And that's where we'll hide your stuff. He told me you can take as much as you can carry."

Under the pile of straw they found several boxes. The markings read: *Wacholder, Vodka* and *Aquavit, Konsumervereinsdestillierungsanstalt GmbH.* "There are twelve to a carton." Elsa tried to give the impression of being well informed. Then she whispered close to Karl's ear, "He's coming back tomorrow, so…"

"Oh good," Karl said loud enough, attempting to dispel any notion of hanky-panky. He turned to Schwarzer. "How many can you take?" He ripped open a box marked Vodka. "We use the cardboard dividers as protection. How many, Schwarzer?"

"Eight, maybe. I think that's all. You can't even take eight in your miserable bags. Safely, I mean."

They opened more boxes and stuffed bottles into their primitive knapsacks, together with straw and cardboard to keep them from rattling.

"I'll stay... make sure everything is... you know, in order. You'd better go ahead..." Karl said as he opened another box. "Kurzer, you know as well as I do... through the moor. Better separate..." Karl stumbled, making no sense. "I'll be right behind you."

Elsa busied herself hiding the canisters and herring cans in the straw. Schwarzer, Kurzer and Hans-Peter stood around, not knowing what to do. They were embarrassed, witnessing what was going on between the girl and Karl. It was too obvious that something was going on.

Hans-Peter nudged Kurzer. "Come on, let's go." Loudly he said, "Sure, we go ahead." He was glad to leave the two lovebirds.

Kurzer, Schwarzer and Hans-Peter went out into the night for the trek back across the border.

"Did you see that? They'll be rolling in the hay from the minute we shut the door behind us." Kurzer shook his head. "And he says Walter is his buddy."

"He's cheating on Krista with that *Rollmops*," Hans-Peter added. "Should we tell her?"

"I wouldn't get involved," said Schwarzer. "Let's keep quiet about it. It's none of our business, and besides, we don't even know for sure."

"Huh! I think it's pretty clear what's going on," answered Hans-Peter. "But I agree. Best to keep our mouths shut."

"Right. Quiet now." Kurzer had taken the lead as they were entering the security zone along the border. "And keep those bottles from clanging."

Manfred awoke the moment Kurzer, Hans-Peter and Schwarzer entered the bungalow. Klaus woke up, too, but Krista slept soundly. Twenty bottles of booze joined all the other contraband behind the partition in the tool room.

"Where's Karl?" Manfred asked in a hushed voice.

"Banging the *Rollmops*. Oops, wasn't supposed to say that."

Hans-Peter caught himself.

"What do you mean?" Klaus asked drowsily.

"Nothing. Forget it. He'll be here in... How long will he take, Kurzer?"

"Will you shut up? He's taking care of something. He'll be here soon."

"Right, taking care of something," Hans-Peter agreed eagerly.

"What's going on?" Krista stirred briefly.

"Nothing. Go back to sleep."

Karl showed up before dawn. He did not say anything and the gang slept, or pretended to be asleep, as he came into the room. He brought four more bottles of Vodka and put them behind the partition. Then he joined Krista on the couch.

***

Heinz was not a bad student. He kept his marks up and passed easily into the next grade. His father did not have to go back to the old sawmill. He found employment as an engineer at the local shipyard that was being dismantled. The remaining parts and machinery were loaded on a vessel bound for England. His work gave him access to items with certain value on the black market: brass hinges, stainless steel fasteners, circuit breakers, turnbuckles—things he could carry away easily hidden in his clothes.

Although he slept at home most nights, Heinz stayed closely in touch with the gang and functioned as a valuable liaison. In the high school he attended, a brisk business was underway during recess between classes. Cigarettes and ration coupons as well as shoes, clothing and fabric, bicycle tires and repair kits, and tools of all kinds changed hands. Most of the contraband liquor from the Russian zone Heinz passed on to distributors, producing great material profits. Money was nearly worthless, especially since rumors of replacing the old Reichsmark with a new currency became increasingly widespread. The question was no longer *if*, but *when*.

"We have to think ahead," said Heinz one evening to Karl as they were sitting alone in front of the bungalow. The weather had been gentle from mid-April on, and the people living in the garden colony began to spend more time outdoors. The boys kept mostly to themselves, but were friendly with their neighbors. "We have to stay ahead of the game. The reform will happen." Heinz was smart, by far the smartest in the Gang of Seven, and he had the most contact with better-educated people through his parents and his school.

"How can we prepare for something we don't know if or when it will happen?" Karl was a good leader, but his intelligence did not rise above average.

"People trade in a lot of their jewelry, just to stay alive. We have the resources to cash in on some of it. Gold, silver, diamonds. I know a couple of guys…"

Kurzer came out of the house. "What are you talking about? Can I get in on it?"

"We're just talking," said Karl. "Of course. No secrets in the Gang, but, as I said: we're just talking."

"Wolfgang Johannsen, you know… He has disappeared. Didn't come back from Berlin. His parents don't know what happened."

"What do you mean, disappeared?" Karl asked.

"That's all I know. His mother says she's going over there to find out."

"That's crazy! Then she's not coming back either," Heinz exploded. "What was he doing in Berlin, anyway?"

"I told you, I don't know."

No one spoke for a while. There were many stories of disappearances in Berlin, interrogations, deportations, but this one came close to home. Actually somebody they knew.

Kurzer said, "His father went to Hamburg to talk to the British liaison officer. He wants them to put pressure on the Russians."

"It can take months until they hear something," said Heinz. "If they find out anything at all," and after a while, "What was he doing in Berlin, I wonder?"

The illegal border crossings became more difficult, the controls on the Russian side better organized. Nevertheless, through the summer of 1947 the Gang continued the excursions, transporting a great variety of merchandise in their newly acquired knapsacks into the Soviet occupation zone, returning with *Schnaps*.

One night in early October, Karl and Kurzer crossed the Wesloer Moor to deliver the two remaining canisters of oil and a knapsack full of laundry powder. Instead of Elsa, Walter met them as they entered the barn. The kerosene lamp shed a flickering light. Kurzer, who had never met Walter, was shocked to find him wearing the green *VoPo* uniform.

"How you doing, Walter," said Karl who was as unprepared for this encounter as Kurzer.

Walter did not answer, but motioned to Kurzer to take off his backpack. "Get out of here. And don't come back, you hear?" Then he turned to Karl. "Take it off, and let's sit down." He led him to a bench, taking the lamp with him. "Leave the pack there, Elsa will take care of it."

Kurzer left the barn and before closing the door behind him, he heard Walter saying, "I had a little talk with Elsa…"

"Not good, not good…" he mumbled to himself, as he walked away from the place. *"It had to come to this."* If they had a fight, Karl would easily win; he was taller, heavier and stronger than Walter. *But Walter wears that green uniform,* Kurzer thought as he made his way alone through the moor.

"So, what do you think will happen now?" Manfred knew as well as the others that their cross-border business was over. "There are only two cans of herring, some marmalade and laundry powder left. But we have a good supply of *Feiner Aquavit* and *Wacholder*. We do not need to risk traversing the no-man's land. We can conduct our business here."

"Yeah, yeah, all right," Hans-Peter cut him short. "You can *conduct* all you want. First of all: What happened to Karl, huh? What do you think Walter will do?"

Nobody knew the answer, but they all had the same suspicion. "Walter in the border police. Who would have thought?" Schwarzer shook his head. "And Karl screwing his girlfriend." Then, as an afterthought, "Now we know why we never met Walter before."

Heinz, who happened to be there, said, "Karl's a good guy, only not too smart."

Krista was quiet. She was probably thinking: *what will happen to me now?*

Quietly Heinz spoke the words that were on everyone's mind. "I don't think we'll see Karl again."

Kurzer asked, "Do any of you think he knew Walter was in the border police?" He looked around. "I guess not."

Kurzer met Herr Johannsen on the street. "Wie gehts, Herr Johannsen? How are you? Any news about Wolfgang?"

"They found out where he is, but they won't tell me. They don't want me to interfere."

"You mean, he's in East Berlin? The KGB have him?"

"We assume that. They don't say exactly. Nothing about where or why."

"Do you know why he was in Berlin?"

"I can't talk about that. I'm not quite sure myself. My wife wanted to go, but they don't let her." He turned to continue on his way. "Espionage... That's what they say."

Kurzer held him by his sleeve. "Karl didn't come back the other night. *VoPo* got him. What do you think will happen?"

"Karl? The one you did that oil thing with?"

"Yeah, him. *VoPo* caught him in... in the Wesloer Moor."

"That's different. That's not Berlin. In Berlin it's always espionage they charge them with. They'll probably let him go in a couple of days." With that he walked away.

I hope so, but I don't think so. Kurzer had not told Herr Johannsen the real story. *Who knows what Walter's intentions are.*

Heinz brought one of the older boys from school to the garden house. "Gerd is the guy I was telling you about," he introduced him to Schwarzer who was alone at home. The others were on some errands. Krista and Klaus went separately to different stores to buy flour, sugar and lard on the extra coupons they had. Schwarzer had taken over the leadership since Karl was missing. He maintained it was temporary.

He and Gerd shook hands. "What have you got for us," Schwarzer opened.

"Depends on what you have for me," Gerd came back

shrewdly. "I can get pretty much anything you want. Watches, rings, you name it. You want a fur coat? I have it. Antiques? A painting?"

Hidden from view behind the partition were over a hundred bottles of booze, but Schwarzer just said, "We have some *Schnaps*. Gin, vodka..."

"That's good currency. That and cigarettes. You have cigarettes?"

"Ein paar Stangen Amis," Schwarzer said vaguely. "A few cartons, American." Over time, a good supply of Phillip Morris and Lucky Strike had accumulated, but there was no need for Gerd to know what and how much they had in storage, at least not yet.

Slowly, as trust grew between them, they came to the point where actual negotiations began and a lucrative business relationship developed. With the border crossings suspended, the inventory of liquor decreased rapidly. Cigarettes were easier to handle, less cumbersome to transport, and their value was more stable.

For their own needs, the Gang had sufficient resources. Kurzer was essentially still the purveyor of vegetables and horsemeat, while the others scrounged whatever was available in food stores on ration cards. Krista developed quite an expertise preparing tasty meals with the supplies she had.

Heinz flourished in his capacity as intermediary. He became an expert in distinguishing genuine from fake or flawed merchandise and Gerd promptly found out who he was dealing with.

Another winter approached. Conditions in the cities had reached intolerable proportions. Clothing was falling apart; shoes were long overdue to be resoled; wood for heating and cooking nearly unobtainable. Even on the black market, many items had become scarce. Some families received CARE packages from relatives in the United States, Denmark or Sweden, containing coffee, cigarettes, lard, chocolate and even clothes and shoes. Most of those precious gifts ended up on the black market to fill other, more pressing needs.

Wolfgang Johannsen and Karl had both disappeared in October. One month passed without word about either one of them.

Herr Johannsen went repeatedly to Hamburg. Every time the officials assured him, "you will hear from us immediately when we know something. He is in custody at the present time and will be released as soon as his innocence is established."

"That's the problem," Herr Johannsen confided in Kurzer. "I don't think he is so innocent. Got mixed up with a group of students in East Berlin. Always planning something, the students."

Kurzer thought of Karl, who was nothing but a small time smuggler. He just made a stupid mistake, betraying his buddy Walter. If Walter decided to hand him over to the occupation authorities, he might yet end up in the hands of the KGB. Then it's endless interrogations, perhaps torture, labor camp, Siberia. *We may never find out.*

***

Hans-Peter, two years older than Klaus and not troubled by ethical concerns, approached Gudrun as she came out of the freight station office. He had seen her from a distance several times after the oil car robbery, but she had no idea who he was.

"Hello, Fräulein, did you just drop this? I couldn't be sure, but it looked like…"

"What? A box of *Pralinen*? I had no chocolate. I didn't drop anything. Where does this come from?" Gudrun was so taken by surprise, she seemed uncertain for a moment. *Me, dropping something? But I had no chocolate. Is this happening?*

The English MPs guarding the freight yard had given her on a few occasions cigarettes, coffee or tea, and only once a small chocolate bar. Those soldiers did not have much themselves, unlike the Americans.

"What is happening here? Who are you and where does this come from?" She looked at the box of chocolates and back at his face. "Where does this come from, huh?"

Hans-Peter showed his charming, mischievous smile. "I could have sworn this fell from your shopping net, but then I thought, can't be. How could she have come by chocolate? And such a beautiful box!" *CADBURY* gleamed in golden letters across the brown and blue box.

Something is going on here, thought the girl. She was not dumb, but intrigued by the approach of this stranger, and by the sight of the chocolate.

Hans-Peter held the box out to her. "Now, that I thought it was yours, you might as well take it. Go ahead."

"Oh no, I couldn't. It would be wrong."

"Tell you what, let's go and sit down over there and talk about this." With that, he steered her by the elbow toward the little café across the cobblestone square on this late afternoon in November. Hans-Peter hid the CADBURY under his short coat. Gudrun walked willingly with him. She gathered her headscarf in front of her face as a gust of snow flurries twirled around them. They entered the café and sat at a small round table.

"Zwei mal *Heissgetränk*," Hans-Peter ordered from the proprietor who came out from behind a swing door, wiping his hands on a dirty apron. "Hot, please," he added, and to the girl, "that will warm us up."

"You had the chocolate, right? You just wanted to talk to me, huh? What a clever gimmick!" She was amused, not annoyed at all, ...*und die Pralinen... I can already taste them!* "What's your name? I think I've seen you around."

"Oh, I am sorry. Hans-Peter. Well, it's a small town."

"I am Gudrun," she said, but he already knew that.

"Oh, Gudrun? That's a pretty name. I like it."

The steaming hot *Heissgetränk* in tall glasses was placed in front of them on the tabletop of cold marble. They both took a sip of the artificially red, artificially fruit-flavored, artificially sweetened liquid.

"So, am I right about the chocolates? Is that how you lure all the girls into your web?"

"Actually... well, yes. I admit it. I wanted to meet you. But no! Not all the girls! I've never done this before. I once saw you coming out of the station."

"I work there."

"I see." Hans-Peter was a good actor, not overplaying his role.

Meanwhile he studied her unobtrusively. She had removed her headscarf and let her black, wavy hair fall loosely to her shoulders. Dark eyes glowed in her pale face. The cold November air had painted red blotches on her cheeks. She wore no lipstick on her thin lips. *Not a bad-looking face*, thought Hans-Peter, *an amusing face. Where can I take her? I definitely want to…*

"What are you looking at? I have a boyfriend, if that's what you're thinking," she interrupted his thoughts.

"Oh no, no! I wasn't thinking anything like that." *A boyfriend? She means Klaus?* "What's your boyfriend's name? Maybe I know him."

"I don't think so. I'd rather not tell." She looked at the chocolates that lay between them on the table.

"Go ahead, open it."

"Really?" She slid one finger under the paper and opened the box, then took one of the mouth watering chocolate candies. "Hmm! Haven't had any chocolate in ages. Take a piece." She pushed the box over to him.

He shook his head. *She took the bait. This babe is mine!* Hans-Peter smiled at her and thought, *I am sure she is talking about Klaus. He can find himself another girl.* "I would like to take you out sometime. You like dancing? They have this band playing all the latest American tunes at *Zum Anker*. Can I pick you up this Thursday?"

Reluctantly at first, Gudrun had said yes. They did go dancing that Thursday, and the next, and they also met at other times. Hans-Peter who had taken up smoking tempted her several times to try it until she gave in. Then, one day he brought a flask of *Aquavit* to their rendezvous at the café and added some of it to their *Heissgetränk*.

She had told him that she lived with her mother. "She's a nurse at a children's hospital, usually on night duty."

The coast was clear. All obstacles were removed. They went dancing, drank *Aquavit* and smoked *Amis*. Gradually he removed Klaus from her mind. In his own mind, Klaus was never an issue.

Gudrun lost her virginity one Thursday night after dancing,

smoking and drinking *Heissgetränk* at *Zum Anker.*

With Karl's fate still uncertain, the remaining members of the Gang still called themselves the Gang of Seven. Kurzer, Manfred and Hans-Peter, with Schwarzer as their *de facto* leader, were the nucleus of the group, although Manfred had found a locksmith with whom he continued his interrupted apprenticeship, and Hans-Peter often seemed to go his separate way. They had an understanding among them not to pry into each other's affairs.

Heinz, though still active and instrumental in the Gang's success, spent more time at his studies. He was one year away from graduating high school.

Klaus had distanced himself somewhat from the activities after the rail car robbery. He continued to see Gudrun although he was aware that she did not let their relationship progress. When he tried to kiss her, she averted her face so that his lips met her cheek instead of her mouth.

He asked her, "Is there something I should know? I thought you liked me."

Gudrun, who was closer to Hans-Peter's age, beat around the bush, but then told him that there was someone else. "I am in love with him. I really think we should not see each other any more."

***

Early December, on a wintry evening, there was a knock at the door of the garden shack. Manfred was studying for his locksmith exam by the dim light of their oil lamp; Hans-Peter and Kurzer interrupted their card game and looked at each other; Schwarzer lowered the magazine he was reading.

Krista, dozing on the sofa, raised her head. "Karl…?" She asked drowsily.

Again a knock at the door, this time more insistent. Schwarzer, seeking approval from his companions, searched their faces. Then he got up. "Who is there?"

"A friend. Let me in, I have information…" answered an unfamiliar voice.

Schwarzer hesitated.

"Go ahead. See who it is," said Manfred who joined Schwarzer at the door. "Ask him who he is and what he wants."

"Who are you and what information are you talking about?"

"Come on, let me in. I'm freezing. I just came from over there."

Manfred nodded, and Schwarzer opened the door just a little. He could not make out the stranger's face in the dark. Gradually he opened the door wider and let the man in. Behind him appeared a girl.

"Thanks. I'm not staying long. Gotta make it back before morning. This is Elsa."

Krista came toward them. "Elsa who? You know something about Karl?"

"Karl was taken away. He had his trial last week and he implicated Walter. Now they have Walter, too. Karl will be free soon, but Walter, that's a different story. Corruption and illegal trafficking, as a member of the police... He's in serious trouble and Elsa fears for her own life. I had to bring her over here." The man was out of breath. "You have something to drink?"

"First tell us who is Elsa." Krista turned to the stove. "You want tea?"

"Tea is fine. Elsa? She's Walter's fiancée. She knows everything. Can she stay with you for a while?" He took the mug of tea from Krista and nodded. "Thanks. We don't think she's safe over there."

Schwarzer was still uncertain about the whole story. "Why did you come here? How did you find us? And tell us your name."

"Karl told me everything before he was taken away." Elsa spoke for the first time. "I know all about the organization, the smuggling, the herring and the booze."

"But there's more to it." The man had still not given them his name. "Walter plays only a small role in a big organization."

"We asked you your name," Manfred asked sharply.

"My name is not important. I go back there and you will never see or hear from me again. Someone will come for Elsa as soon as it is safe for her to return."

"Why so mysterious," Manfred insisted.

"Let's just say, I am in danger myself. The KGB has a long arm. The less you know, the better for you."

"So, you are working underground against the occupation? Against the KGB?" It was Manfred again who asked the question.

"And why did Karl get involved?" Krista wanted to know. "He was only..."

The man cut her off. "That was a personal matter between him and Walter."

"Why don't you sit over there, Krista, and let us handle this," Schwarzer told her gently. She was still not fully aware why Karl had not returned that night six weeks ago and what role Elsa played in this quagmire.

"I don't understand any of this." Krista went to sit on the couch. "When will they let Karl go? And when can he come home?"

"About coming back here... I don't know. They will keep a sharp eye on him. Anybody who has been in their hands will never again be completely free." The man set down his empty tea mug, gave Elsa an encouraging pat on the back and turned to the door. "I have to go. Thanks for the tea." To Elsa he said, "you will be safe here until someone comes for you."

A cold breeze came through the open door as the stranger walked out into the night.

Karl, held at the official border crossing of Helmstedt, awaited the arrival of an exchange prisoner from the western checkpoint. The sun was shining bright and the snow on the sides of the highway was melting. Exactly at the hour of noon, two American soldiers in helmets and with MP armbands on the sleeves delivered a man in civilian clothes. Papers were signed and passed between a Soviet officer, a German *VoPo* captain and the Americans. Karl was taken into custody by the MPs and the civilian was handed over to the eastern authorities. Within minutes Karl reached the US checkpoint from where, after some formalities, he was released and free to travel.

Karl arrived at the garden house a week after the stranger had brought Elsa there.

"I believe you, and frankly, I don't give a damn what happened between you and him." Krista was not angry with Elsa. She had suspected something like this all along, but always suppressed the thought.

"We had sex a few times and that was it. Then Walter found out about it. He broke up with me and reported Karl on illegal trafficking, the contraband, you know. Karl, to save his skin, informed on Walter's activities in the underground movement. Now he is jailed and under investigation. Karl is a good guy," Elsa went on, "but he is nothing to me. Walter is mean and vengeful. I am glad I'm rid of him. He's in for a long time, maybe Siberia. A lot of people have been picked up since."

"I said I believe you. Karl is very good to me. I forgive him. And you."

"He is lucky they made that exchange."

And so the two girls became friends. Karl was taciturn about the whole matter. He treated Krista kindly, was indifferent toward Elsa and did not talk about his ordeal while in custody. All he said to Kurzer, the last one to see him two months earlier, was that he had been interrogated repeatedly by both German and Soviet authorities.

He told Schwarzer the same. "I am glad to be back, but you keep doing what there is to do. I won't interfere. The interzonal business is over; soon all smuggling and black marketing will be over. That's what everybody says. Who knows…"

Karl was referring to the expected monetary reform. That was a foregone conclusion, but the date it was to happen remained a secret.

Schwarzer told him of the change in strategy of the Gang of Seven. "We are accumulating jewelry. Gold and silver, you know. Bracelets, chains, watches. We even have some wedding bands and diamond rings."

Manfred came over to them. "Karl, we have some problem dividing the treasure fairly among us. Heinz thinks he should have a greater share because he facilitated the business partnership with Gerd. Klaus has all but dropped out from our activities. Kurzer and I do what we can, but you know, I am studying for my bachelor's exam, and Hans-Peter is not doing much these days, since he's seeing this girl."

"Wait a minute. Who is Gerd? Klaus dropped out? And what girl are you talking...?"

"Shhh. Not so loud," Schwarzer cautioned.

Klaus heard his name. "I didn't drop out. I am here, am I not? And Hans-Peter is seeing a girl?" *Oh, so that's what it is. He's seeing Gudrun. I knew something was going on there.* "Since when did you know this, Manfred? It's Gudrun, huh? Why didn't you tell me?"

"Okay, let's all be calm here. We must not let this get out of hand." Schwarzer was always the mediator. He stood with Karl, Manfred and Klaus near the stove. Krista and Elsa sat on the sofa. Hans-Peter and Kurzer were out, Heinz probably at his parents. "If it's true that Hans-Peter went behind your back and took Gudrun from you, he will have to deal with me. I do not tolerate misdeeds like that. Karl, what do you say?"

Before Karl answered, Klaus said, "It doesn't concern any of you. Let me handle it." He felt humiliated. "I will confront him and deal with him. This is my business."

I disagree," said Schwarzer. "We are like a family. It affects all of us."

"Schwarzer, you take care of it. Let's get back to the jewelry. But first tell me who is Gerd?" Karl wanted to stay out of the personal affair between Hans-Peter and Klaus.

"Heinz brought Gerd to us. He deals in all that gold and silver," Schwarzer explained. "You will meet him soon. The guy is okay, kind of educated, classy. Shrewd too."

"How much is there?"

"In value? That's hard to say. We hide it behind the partition. Come, I show you." Schwarzer took him aside and they went to the storage area.

"A lot has happened in these two months, huh? You make the most sense here, Schwarzer. Tell me all you know."

"Things have changed, Karl. We have only a few bottles of booze left. Almost everything has been traded in for items of lasting value. Manfred is right, there is a problem with the distribution.

We have to see what happens when the new money replaces the Reichsmark."

"As you said a minute ago: we're like a family. We have to split it evenly. Nobody gets more and nobody gets less. There must be a few thousand marks in this stuff."

***

Klaus waited on one side of the terminal building, partially hidden in the fading light of late afternoon. He had left the garden shack and followed Hans-Peter at a distance. He wanted to catch him and Gudrun together, not to start a fight but to confront them.

Gudrun came out of the office and Hans-Peter gave her a light kiss on the lips; then they crossed the plaza to the café. Klaus stepped out from the shadow of the building and called out, "Hans-Peter, Gudrun!"

As they turned, Klaus caught up with them. He addressed Hans-Peter in a quivering voice, trying to control his emotion. "I knew we were never real friends, but now we are enemies." He had thought it over and over the night before, what to say. He had rehearsed it, but now his voice almost failed him.

Gudrun said, "Klaus..." but he had already turned and walked away.

Klaus decided to leave the Gang. It was no longer the close-knit family it had been. After Karl's disappearance, the dealings with Gerd and the new black market strategies had made it difficult for him to be useful. He was not as smart as Heinz, not as clever and inventive as the others. Schwarzer protected him and that made him feel humiliated. Since the break-in at the fish cannery and the train robbery, his contribution to the Gang was minimal. The new situation between him and Hans-Peter made it impossible for him to stay on. Besides, now that Heinz went back to school and lived with his parents, he was the youngest among them.

Since he had escaped from the Soviet POW camp together with Manfred and Hans-Peter, there had been a certain bond between them. That bond was now broken. For two and a half years Klaus had not given much thought to going back to Hannover to his mother. There had been no closeness in his family, and so the Gang of Seven had become his family.

As a young child, Klaus had observed his parents insulting each other and more than once he had seen his father hitting his mother. He was relieved when early in the war his father was drafted into the *Wehrmacht*. In the spring of 1940 his father was declared missing during the campaign in France and his mother brought into the house another man, an official in the Nazi party. They did not suffer from the shortages of food as the rest of the population, but Klaus was completely neglected. He was sixteen when his troop of Hitler Youths became part of the *Volkssturm* in April of 1945. Three weeks later the Russians took him prisoner as he was hiding in a burned-out building in Berlin.

The day he found out that Hans-Peter had betrayed him and taken Gudrun from him, he made up his mind to go back to Hannover.

This was the beginning of the end of the Gang of Seven.

***

Hans-Peter came home late in the evening. Schwarzer stood up, said to Heinz who was just leaving, "stay for a while," and stopped Hans-Peter at the door.

"Let's go outside for a moment." He put his coat over his shoulders and caught Hans-Peter at the elbow, leading him back out the door. "What's this I hear about you and this girl, Klaus' girl, Gudrun?"

Schwarzer pushed the door closed. They stood just outside, facing each other.

"Gudrun? What about her? What is this, a damned tribunal?" Hans-Peter immediately went on the offensive. "Look, Schwarzer, this has nothing to do with you, so you better stay out of it."

"Let me put it this way: it has everything to do with me and all of us. This group cannot function if there is animosity among us. You have been disloyal to one of us and that means you have been disloyal to all of us. Why couldn't you get your own girl?"

"Oh, come on, leave me alone. What's the big deal?"

"Our Gang is in a crisis already anyway. You just made it worse. I will suggest that you be expelled. We will put it to a vote." With that Schwarzer left Hans-Peter standing outside and went back into the bungalow.

Hans-Peter lit a cigarette and walked slowly through the colony. Fifteen minutes later he returned and entered their dwelling. He acted as if all of this were a joke. "So, have you guys reached a verdict? Am I under arrest, on trial or already convicted? What's it gonna be? Siberia? Concentration camp? Are you the KGB or the Gestapo? Huh, smells like old times."

Karl spoke now. "You have anything to say? We are not the Gestapo or the KGB."

"What do you want me to say? I'm sorry? Forgive me please, for I have sinned? Shit like that? Man, I like this girl and she likes me. For now. Maybe later Klaus can have her back!" He forced a laugh. "If he's man enough."

Klaus got up.

Schwarzer said, "Sit down," and Klaus obeyed. They were all there, but in the dim light no one could see the anger in Klaus' face.

Karl stepped forward. "Hans-Peter and Klaus do not vote. They are the opposing parties in this case. The rest of us vote by a show of hands. Ready?"

Hans-Peter was standing with his back to the door, Karl and Schwarzer stood in the middle of the room; all the others, including the girls, were sitting.

"Who is in favor of expelling Hans-Peter from the Gang of Seven?"

Six hands went up.

"All those against?"

Manfred raised his arm. "Out of loyalty to my old friend and partner, my fellow escapee from the clutches of the Red Army, I stand by him, although he has betrayed one of us." In his stilted manner of speaking, Manfred explained his position. "Damn you, Hans-Peter, you did wrong, but I cannot go against you."

All were silent for a moment, for they had not anticipated an emotional outburst from anyone. They also had not thought about what to do now. Was he to leave right away? Send him out into the cold night? Give him another chance to say something? What about his share of the treasure, the asset, as they called it?

After a while, Schwarzer said quietly, "Pack your stuff and leave, Hans-Peter. Sorry it had to come to this."

"Want me to go with you? I just have to get my coat." They were standing outside the door in the chilly night. "Where will you go? Not good for you to walk out alone in the night. We can go to the bus station, hang out. At least we'd not be out on the street." Manfred has always been closest to Hans-Peter and he didn't want their friendship to end abruptly. Hans-Peter had gathered his few belongings and stuffed shirts, underwear, socks and a pair of pants into this knapsack. He wore his army coat.

"No. Thanks. I'll see if I can get Gudrun to let me in. I hope her mother isn't there. I've never met her mother."

Manfred assured him that he would take care of his share of the asset hidden away in the old chest behind the partition. "The Gang is breaking up. We will have to divide it among us soon and you have to get your share. I'll see to it."

"Thanks, man. I'll let you know where you can find me." He walked away and the night swallowed him. Shivering, Manfred returned into the house.

They were all quiet. What was there to say? Years of comradeship... slipping away. They did not know it would be so emotional.

"We are still the Gang of Seven—with one missing," Karl broke the silence. "You were the Gang of Seven when I was... when I wasn't here."

Karl had not assumed the leadership again since he came back from his two months in custody in the Russian zone. Schwarzer had taken over and Karl wanted it to stay that way. Heinz was still an active member, although not full time, living with his parents and preparing for his high school diploma. Manfred was an apprentice at a locksmith's in town; he spent fewer hours with the Gang. Kurzer was forever roaming the gardens and stores, scrounging for food items he could find and bringing in the occasional chunk of horsemeat. Elsa had joined the group but, like Krista, was not considered a member of the Gang. That left Klaus, and he was leaving for good.

Gerd, the expert in goods of lasting value, was recognized only as an affiliate, not a member, and they trusted him with some reservation. Heinz had made the connection with him and proposed the change in the Gang's strategy. Gerd remained an outsider, but he was essential to the survival of the Seven beyond the impending economic upheaval, even though the Gang as such would not last. They could not imagine how the monetary reform would affect them. The uncertainty was on everyone's mind and they felt the glue that held them together was losing its grip.

There was no doubt that Gerd made a good profit in all their dealings. On the evening before Klaus took his departure, the Gang gathered for a serious discussion. Heinz had brought Gerd, but Schwarzer declared, "This is an internal conference of our group. Members only. So, if you don't mind, we would like to have this discussion among ourselves. We will let you know anything that might be of concern to you."

"I understand," said Gerd, slick as he was, and left.

"I'll be in touch," Heinz called after him before the door closed.

"Karl, would you like to say something?" Schwarzer addressed him. They still respected Karl as their former leader, although he no longer involved himself in the decision-making.

Karl's features could scarcely be discerned as he stood behind the table from which the oil lamp emitted a flickering light. He spoke in a quiet tone. "I was never elected by you, so I never had to formerly resign. I know you trusted me and still do. So, let me just say this: the Gang of Seven has survived for two and a half years and is now about to dissolve. We will have to integrate ourselves into mainstream society. Big changes are ahead. I propose, and intend to keep our friendship, to help each other where help is needed, but we have to find our individual ways." After a pause he added, "I declare the Gang of Seven terminated as of this evening." He sat down.

A long silence followed his short speech. At last Schwarzer, without getting up from where he sat, cleared his throat. "Nothing has to change immediately. We're still here. The owner hasn't claimed the bungalow. But changes are coming and we have to be prepared. First of all, I propose to distribute the assets among us and that is why I did not want Gerd here. Now, this will not be easy. Heinz, you have kept a list of value in cigarettes of the individual items, right?"

"Not exactly. Some of the items came in package deals, so I don't know what we paid for all the individual pieces of jewelry."

"We will have to estimate, and I need everyone's cooperation. The basic currency is the cigarette. Four marks the equivalent of a *Sondermischung*, seven for *Lucky Strike, Chesterfield* and so on, also for the English *Players, Wild Woodbine, Craven A* and *Senior Service*. Any questions so far?"

"Hans-Peter will have to get his share. I gave him my word to make sure he gets it," said Manfred.

"Any objections?"

Klaus gave a snort, but made no comment.

"Okay. We will do this tomorrow morning. We need daylight." Schwarzer was glad there was no resistance. "Karl, you will see to it that Krista is not overlooked, huh?"

"I'll take care of her," Karl nodded. He shifted his eyes over to Elsa. "You will have to go back over there. Is anyone coming for you?"

"I don't want to go back. Can I stay with you, Krista? Wherever you go?"

Krista looked at Karl who answered for her.

"You have to go back. I am sorry, but there is no place for you here. I'll take you myself, if no one comes to get you."

Elsa started sobbing quietly. Krista gave her a hug. "It's gonna be all right."

Oh shit, why did she ever come here? "Sorry, Elsa," Schwarzer said softly. "Your place is with your father. That's more than any of us can say." He went behind the partition and came back with a bottle of *Wacholder*.

"Let us drink to the good fortune we had these years of finding each other and forming this friendship that will last into the future." He extracted the cork and poured a generous measure into their mugs. "We came through hard times together." He continued, as if talking to himself, "We must break with the past and contemplate what lies ahead. We all carry something... It's how we deal with it." He raised his mug. "We must move on." No more words came from his lips. Bitter memories of his youth flooded his mind. With the burning elixir he swallowed the emotions of the moment together with those of his past and then with the back of his hand wiped away any tears that might have come to his eyes.

They drank silently. Karl got up to refill the mugs. "Come on, you guys, it's not the end of the world. It's a new beginning. Cheers." They drank and then Manfred grabbed the bottle and filled the mugs one more time. "To our comrade Hans-Peter. He has failed us, but once he was a friend."

Some more reluctant than others, they all emptied their cups.

PART TWO

The sudden change in June of 1948 jump-started the new German economy and the normalization of living conditions. Everyone began a new life with forty deutsch marks the day the new currency was introduced. The road was paved for the miraculous West German rise to an important European industrial nation and global trading partner.

Great difficulties had yet to be overcome. In August of 1961, to stem the massive exodus from the *DDR* to the west, the East German government ordered the building of the ninety-six mile-long Berlin Wall, which cut Berlin in two, until it was breached and torn down in November of 1989.

The western sectors of Berlin lived through the blockade and the most extraordinary airlift in history. The establishment of the *Deutsche Demokratische Republik*, the *DDR* incorporated the eastern sector of Berlin and separated the Soviet-occupied eastern part of Germany from the allied zones in the west.

In 1949, Konrad Adenauer became the first Chancellor of West Germany and he led the new Federal Republic until 1963.

MEATLOAF
AND
DIAMONDS

The Johannsens had not heard from their son Wolfgang for more than five years when a distant relative sent them a clipping from an East Berlin newspaper. In a photograph, a man exits a building and heads for a black sedan. The caption read: **W. Johannsen leaving Stasi headquarters after conference with Soviet/German officials yesterday.**

Herr Johannsen put on his glasses and read the attached note: *Ist dies Euer Wolfgang?*

"Yes, that's him," he said to his wife. "Take a look. Need the magnifying glass? I am sure it's him. Look at his posture."

"Our Wolfgang? What's he doing with the *Stasi*, the *Staats Sicherheitsdienst*?" After years of getting nowhere with the western authorities, they had given up hope. "He's not in Siberia? Imprisoned or—you know?"

They had just come to terms with the tragic fate that they had lost their only son, and now the old wound was ripped open again. "But it's him, you see?" said her husband.

"Yes, I see. He's alive! How do we get him back? He can't be over there on his own free will. You think he's with the East German Secret Police? That's impossible."

"We don't know anything. Maybe they brainwashed him. Maybe... He did act a little strange, remember?"

"I can still feel that last hug he gave me. Different... Almost as if he wanted to tell me something."

"I'll take this to Hamburg tomorrow. They must know about this. I'll raise hell if they don't talk to me. Believe me!"

Frau Johannsen was at Butcher Timm's to buy ground beef and ground pork for the meatloaf she was going to prepare for supper. Ulli Bolt attended her.

"Half a pound of each, Frau Johannsen? Here we go." He looked at her. "There is something on your mind, huh? What's the good news?"

"Ach wissen Sie... We don't know anything yet, but..." She whispered across the counter, "we heard from Wolfgang—not directly, but he's alive. My husband is in Hamburg to find out more."

"How so, Frau Johannsen? Did he call? Where is he?"

No other customers were in the store; still they spoke in hushed voices, as if afraid to be overheard. "There was a picture in the paper... an East Berlin paper. I can't tell you more just now."

Ulli Bolt was puzzled. "What do you mean? He's—in the East?"

"We don't know. We are so afraid... for him, you know."

A customer entered the store and Ulli spoke in his natural tone. "Here you are, Frau Johannsen. Five hundred grams. Thank you. Have a nice evening." He added in a whisper, "may I stop by later?"

"Your son, Herr Johannsen, is a defector. You have to understand, there is nothing we can do to bring him back. Had he been kidnapped, we would be able to assert pressure, but... Herr Johannsen, your son has decided to join them. There is nothing we can do."

Dejected and confused, he left the British embassy in Hamburg. His feelings were mixed. Wolfgang was alive, but they would not be able to get in touch with him, unless he changed his mind, came to his senses and returned home.

***

Karl Berger and Manfred Scholte were the first ones of the old Gang of Seven to find lodgings in town. From the time they had left the garden colony, they became closer friends than they had been as members of the Gang.

When the Gilberts showed up to claim their property, only Schwarzer and Kurzer still occupied the garden house. Herr Gilbert found the house in good condition and made no demands other than to vacate it.

Kurt Lansen, formerly known as Schwarzer, had managed to be accepted at the *Wirtschaftsakademie* in Hamburg and returned after two years to Schlutup with a teaching degree in business. He held an associate position at the local *Handelschule*.

Karl Berger had been able to rebuild the one-story house in which he had lived with his parents. It was heavily damaged in the air raid of April 1942 on the town of Schlutup. He made it livable again while occupying the basement until the roof was repaired.

Kurzer helped him often in the evenings and on the weekends. The building in which he grew up had been destroyed in the same bombing attack that damaged Karl's house. Kurzer's mother had died in the explosion.

Karl worked in a construction firm. The housing shortage and neglect during the war years made construction—better called re-construction—one of the most profitable enterprises. Karl often worked twelve hours a day and then had numerous requests for re-pair jobs on the weekends.

"Your last name is Bolt, right?" Karl asked his young friend one day. "I knew your parents." He was not sure of Kurzer's first name; they had always called him Kurzer.

"You don't know my first name, huh? Would you call me by my first name if I told you?"

"Sure, if you like. What is it?"

"It's Ulrich; you can call me Ulli."

"So, how's it going, Ulli? Butcher Timm treating you all right?"

"He's a good man. He wants me to stay on after my bachelor's exam."

As an apprentice, Ulli Bolt attended the Handelschule twice weekly, a requirement to graduate from apprenticeship. Kurt was his teacher in the simple practices of things like carrying a ledger of debits and credits.

Manfred Scholte finished his apprenticeship, made a good living as a locksmith, but he had his eyes on more than fixing broken locks and replacing lost keys. He had a keen sense of where money could be made: tools and accessories, household gadgets, paints and cleaning products. There was a never-ending demand for repair kits and materials. He explored and developed his contacts with suppliers in the locks and gadgets field and managed to gradually take over the small shop from his aging boss and expand it into a hardware store.

Renting a room in the house of an elderly couple, he fell in love with the landlord's granddaughter. Manfred was twenty-five years old when he asked the girl to marry him; she was only sixteen at the time. Her grandfather insisted that she be at least eighteen before he would agree to the marriage, but Manfred and Frieda, the girl, didn't want to wait that long and they ran away together for one night in a hotel. When they came back, the old folks insisted for them to be wed. That settled, the young couple moved into a newly renovated apartment on the outskirts of town.

One leisurely Sunday evening, Karl and Manfred sat on the balcony that attached to Karl's living room, drinking cool Pilsners. Krista and Frieda were in the kitchen.

"Once Hans-Peter left the Gang, the atmosphere in the house changed dramatically, no Karl? Wouldn't you say so, huh? He was a bad influence, disturbed the harmony, huh?" Manfred had not lost his fondness for words. "He was my friend ever since we met in the POW camp, escaped together and made it through to the west. But he ruined it. He had that irresponsible, care-about-nothing attitude. Damn, he had to ruin it."

"Yeah, you are right. He had a bad streak. When did you last hear from him? Wasn't he trying to get into the *Bundeswehr*?"

"He did get in. Was in training to drive a *Panzer*, he told me.

But that's almost a year ago and I don't know if that's true." Manfred leaned closer to Karl. "Hey Karl, none of my business, but... tell me, when are you going to get... you know, married?"

At that moment Ulli Bolt showed up. "Hey, you guys. Guess what: Frau Johannsen came into the store the other day. She told me they heard from Wolfgang. Not directly, though; they had a picture of him from an East Berlin paper. He's in East Berlin." Ulli pulled up a chair and joined them.

"In East Berlin?" Manfred was incredulous.

Karl leaned toward him, "What are you saying? What kind of picture? Go, ask Krista for a beer; she'll give you a cool one."

"I don't know. They had a picture of him, cut from an East Berlin paper." He got up to get a beer from Krista. Back on the balcony, he said. "I went to see them that evening after work. His father had just come back from Hamburg. At the embassy they couldn't help him. He went over there voluntarily, they told him."

"What do you mean? He's on the other side? All these years they knew nothing, and now he turns up in East Berlin?" Manfred still didn't get it.

"Yeah, that's about it. He's an agent with the *Stasi*, if you asked me. A spy."

"He's always been a shifty character. Remember? He made a big fuss over helping us with that material for our backpacks," said Karl and added, "I never liked him."

Frieda came out to them. "Dinner's ready. Come and eat."

Krista had set the table in the kitchen. "Ulli, you're staying with us?"

"Okay, thanks." He has never had much luck with girls and he was still single and unattached.

They sat down to eat. "You heard that, Krista?"

"Heard what?"

"About Wolfgang. Tell her, Ulli."

Ulli wasn't a good talker, especially with one of the opposite sex. He just said, "Wolfgang. He's in the east."

"Yeah, so? What does than mean: he's in the east? You mean the *DDR*, right?"

"No, girl," Karl took up the conversation. "He's in East Berlin, with the *Stasi*."

"You're talking about Wolfgang Johannsen, right? I never met him."

"That's not the point. He used to be one of us. Well, not exactly, but now he's over there. He defected."

"Pass me the potatoes. Help yourselves to the meat. There's cauliflower. This thing with that guy don't mean nothin' to me. Frieda, get the gravy; it's still on the stove."

Krista was not interested in things that went on outside her immediate surrounding, so they dropped that subject and dedicated themselves to the meal. At least she was a good cook.

After the meal, the guys sat again on the balcony while the women cleaned up inside.

"Any of you heard from Klaus lately?" Ulli wanted to know.

Klaus Lietke had left Schlutup in the spring of 1948, after the incident with his girlfriend Gudrun and Hans-Peter. He had sent two letters the first year and then they lost contact. They knew he was going back to school, but that was so long ago.

"Not a word," Manfred answered as they enjoyed the mild evening on the balcony, drinking their beer. "Last I heard was he lived with his mother, but the man she'd been with, that Nazi, you know, he was gone. Either they caught him or he ran to Argentina or something."

"And Heinz Kluge," said Karl, "he's gonna be all right. He is very smart. When his father got that job back in Cologne and they moved several years ago, he told me he was going to study chemistry at the university of Bonn."

"He was the smartest of us all," Manfred agreed. "Without him we might have never gone into that business with the jewelry. We would have been penniless when the deutsch mark... you know."

"That reminds me of Gerd. Anybody know what happened to him?" Ulli looked from Manfred to Karl. "I did not like him. An arrogant bastard, he was."

"Nobody liked him, but we needed him," said Karl. "I have no idea where he is now."

Manfred nodded his agreement. "I don't know either." He got

up. "Is there another beer, Karl? Can we have one more?"

"Help yourself—and bring us one, too."

Gerd had disappeared from Schlutup. Like Heinz, he passed the Abitur, the German high school diploma. They knew he had lived with some relatives of his, but since the new economy was set in motion in June of 1948, nobody had heard from him.

***

Gerd Schenker surfaced in Frankfurt. Sitting at a round table in the café at the *Hauptwache*, he was having a discussion with two gentlemen. All three, dressed in respectable business suits, gave the impression of serious businessmen or brokers at the nearby *Börse*, the Frankfurt stock exchange.

The café was not crowded at this hour before lunchtime and their conversation was carried on in low voices. One of the gentlemen nodded at the clock on the opposite wall. "She'll be here any minute now," he said and then signaled the waiter to bring over another chair. "We are expecting someone to join us shortly."

The waiter busied himself collecting the dishes. "Is there anything else, gentlemen?"

Gerd said, "Three brandies please. That will be all for now. Thank you."

A few minutes after the waiter had added another chair to their table, removed the dishes and brought the brandies, a stylishly dressed young woman entered the café and walked confidently toward them. Gerd stood up and the other two followed, but she gestured for them to remain seated. The waiter pulled out the chair for her and she sat down. Gerd began to introduce her, when she interrupted.

"My name is not important and I don't need to know your names. You will never see me again after today." She nodded toward Gerd. "I have met Herr Schenker."

The waiter stood at a discrete distance and Gerd gave him the signal to bring one more brandy.

"I have to leave promptly for my flight back to London," she said. "I understand you have something for my associates there."

"Of course." The man sitting on Gerd's left removed a padded envelope from his breast pocket and slid it across the table. There was no secrecy in his doing so, but to a seasoned observer it might have seemed excessively open, as if to dispel the notion of a covert transaction. "You may look inside to be sure it is to your satisfaction."

One look under the open flap was enough for her to see it contained at least three dozen large, medium and smaller diamonds. She dipped her napkin in the brandy, moistened the flap with it and sealed the envelope, then placed it in her elegant briefcase and handed Gerd a plain white envelope. A quick examination told him it contained a bank check for one point two million pounds.

The young woman sipped some of the brandy and then gave a small indication of a smile. "I thank you for the brandy," and after a look at her wristwatch, "I must be on my way." She nodded a short good-bye and got up.

Gerd accompanied her leaving the café, summoned a taxi for her and then returned to the table. "Let's go."

The waiter pocketed the generous amount of money left for him and bowed as they went out through the revolving door. Gerd walked to the parking garage to retrieve his car, while the others signaled for taxis, one heading in the direction of the Palm Garden, the other along Kaiserstrasse.

After the stylishly dressed young woman passed customs at Heathrow airport, a stranger met her and escorted her to a waiting *Mini*. Both slid into the backseat and the driver headed for a northern suburb of London.

The following day her partially nude body was found by the side of a rarely traveled rural road. She had been strangled with one of her own nylon stockings. There was no briefcase and no ID.

German newspapers reported two seemingly unrelated gang style slayings, one in West Berlin, the other at the Helmstedt border crossing.

Days later, Gerd Schenker opened an anonymous account at a Zurich bank in the amount of one point two million pounds sterling.

***

Heinz Kluge sat at the desk in his apartment in Bonn. He had the habit of leaving the television on while he studied. He had the rare ability to pay attention to more than one thing at a time.

A news item distracted him from his studies. "A significant portion of the diamonds stolen in Johannesburg, South Africa, six months ago turned up in a storage facility in the port city of Hull, England. One man, thought to be a member of an international jewelry theft ring, was arrested..." Heinz lost interest until he heard, "anyone with information regarding the whereabouts of Gerd Schenker of West Germany..." He saw the mug shot, frontal and profile. There was no doubt it was Gerd, although he had aged quite a bit since Heinz had last seen him.

Heinz, who had not been in touch with any of his old friends for some time, located the slip of paper on which he had once scribbled a phone number. He dialed.

"Herr Schenker, bitte?"

"You must have a wrong number. There is nobody here by that name."

I thought so, said Heinz to himself and replaced the receiver in its cradle.

Frau Kluge, Heinz' mother, heard the name Schenker on the car radio as she drove home from her volunteer job at the library. *Schenker*, she thought. *Gerd Schenker—isn't that the name of that friend of Heinz? The one we didn't like? The police looking for him? I'm not surprised.*

From home she called her son. "Heinz, did you hear that? Could that be Gerd Schenker, your friend from high school?"

"I saw his photo on the TV. It's him. Has to do with a diamond theft. He is very smart, you know. They will have a hard time finding him."

"Heinz, I am concerned about you. You were friends."

"Mom, I haven't seen him or heard from him for years. What are you talking about?"

"Okay. I just thought... You know, we never liked you to hang out with him."

Mothers, Heinz mumbled as he hung up. *I really never liked him either.*

Gerd, his criminal mind fully developed and combined with an extraordinary intelligence, had his future planned well in advance. With Interpol on his heels for grand larceny and suspicion of homicide, European soil had become too hot for him. Using several aliases he made his way via Pakistan, Indonesia and New Zealand to Montevideo, Uruguay, where he settled under the name of Günter Neumann.

***

Hans-Peter was among the first to enlist in the new army of the Federal Republic of Germany at its inception in 1949. Different from the old Prussian *Kadavergehorsam*, blind obedience, he found the less stringent regulations of the new *Bundeswehr* more to his liking. Discipline was not one of his virtues.

His motorized unit was stationed near a small village in Bavaria where he heard the news that the police was looking for Gerd Schenker. He called his old friend Manfred, the only one with whom he had remained in contact once every other month or so.

"Hey, Manfred, how's it going? How's the hardware business?"

"Hans-Peter, how are you? How's the army treating you?"

"All right, so far. Listen, I heard in the news they're looking for that guy we did business with, you know, with the jewelry. Gerd Schenker—wasn't that his name?"

"That's him, all right. What... You know where he is? If you do, don't tell me. I don't want any part of that."

"No, no. I have no idea. Just checking if you had heard about it. You mean... Could we be in trouble?"

"I don't think so, but you never know. I keep my distance from those who live beyond the law."

"Hey, still got that fancy talk, huh? Listen, if you hear something, let me know."

"I will in no way get involved or even talk about it. I am a model citizen, living a quiet life, a married man, minding my own business. I closed the door on the past. You'd better do the same. Stay out of trouble." He laughed, "I know that's hard for you, but try your best."

"Does Heinz know? They were close friends, you know."

"I don't know. Let's not talk about it anymore."

"Right. I gotta go."

Kurt Lansen had recently married his girlfriend Ilse. On a Sunday, the young couple paid Karl and Krista a visit, as they often did. It had been months since they last heard anything about the diamond robbery, the homicide of the two men and the search for Gerd Schenker. Their treasure—their assets, as they called it—had been disposed of in the first weeks after the turnover to the deutsch mark, more than ten years ago. That had nothing to do with this year's diamond heist in South Africa; still, the subject came up among the friends; they felt they were in some distant way connected with it.

"Gerd Schenker—no wonder... A fugitive from the police. An international fugitive!"

"A celebrity!" Karl added. "You know, I was always a little in awe of him. He had something, can't put my finger on it. Super intelligent, but sinister. He must be twenty-eight, twenty-nine years old now. Did you see him on TV? Those must be his passport photos."

"Will they catch him?" asked Ilse. "I did not know him, but what I get from the way you are talking about him, he's a slick one."

"Ah, he's gone," said Karl. "He is too smart for them."

Kurt was skeptical. "They might even want to ask us some questions."

"What for? We don't know anything. Maybe Heinz... Do you have his number?"

"Listen, both of you," Ilse interrupted. "The less you know, the better. Don't go around asking questions, getting in touch with everybody, showing so much interest. Don't draw attention."

"She's right, Kurt. You got a smart wife. It's in the past. Let's forget about it."

"Right, Krista," Ilse agreed with her. "Will you forget it? It does not concern you. You once knew the guy, that's all. You act as if you were involved in the crime."

"All right, all right; let's drop it," Kurt gave in to his wife.

"So, what's on your mind, Ulli?" Karl repeated. "You looked like you had something on your mind when you came in."

"Yeah." He paused. "Herr Timm wants to retire. Wants me to take over the shop. I don't know..."

"You see? He mentioned it to me last week," Kurt exclaimed. "He wants you to become *Meister*, right? Man, Ulli, you've got it made! *Schlachtermeister* Ulrich Bolt! How does that sound, huh?"

"You think I can do it? I don't know if I can."

"Sure, why not? Karl chimed in. "That's a reason to celebrate."

"No. Not yet, anyway." Ulli was hesitant, so unsure of himself. "Let me think this over. Kurt, would you help me with the preparation? There is so much I have to know for the exam. It's not easy. The regulations, the health inspections, payroll and taxes..."

"I'll work with you. You will become *Schlachtermeister*, believe me." Kurt put his hands on Ulli's shoulders. "Trust me."

***

Klaus Lietke did not finish high school. In Hannover he went back to school, but did not achieve more than what was then called the *mittlere Reife,* an intermediate high school certificate. At age nineteen he applied for a job at the local grocery market. A new invention in convenient shopping had just reached the German economy. Little family stores, greengrocers, fish markets, butcher shops and neighborhood bakeries were soon driven out of existence. *Supermarkets*, they called them, and Klaus had found his niche. From storeroom attendant to cashier to supervisor, he climbed to the position of manager.

He was satisfied with his success, although his mother never stopped nagging him for not attaining a more prestigious position. He had long put aside his memories of Gudrun and Hans-Peter; he had moved on and, when he turned twenty-five, he asked his girlfriend, Helga, to marry him. Helga worked in the produce section of the supermarket. She was a bright girl, but her ambition did not go beyond doing a good job at the store and her mind was set at becoming a wife and a mother.

Klaus Lietke, promoted to manager of three stores in the greater Hannover area, was married and father of two girls by the time he was twenty-seven years old.

News about the police looking for Gerd Schenker had reached him too, but he did not want to give it much thought. He remembered the three years in Schlutup—the smuggling, the black marketeering, the struggle to survive—with a mix of nostalgia and reluctance.

He had told Helga of his friends Karl and Schwarzer, "They were older than me, had a lot of experience in the war and stuff. They kind of looked out for me. When that with Hans-Peter happened, they were all on my side, even Manfred."

Klaus made an annoyed gesture, as if trying to dismiss an unpleasant memory. "I left before June of '48 with some of the… we called it our 'asset'. It was all legit; I mean, no crime was committed, but I felt like a criminal with that jewelry in my knapsack."

"But who is this Gerd Schenker? He wasn't one of your gang, right?"

"He was a friend of Heinz. An evil character. Nobody liked him."

He did not want to talk about it anymore and Helga understood. "But he got you started, Klaus. You and your mother wouldn't have had anything. Maybe we wouldn't have met either. Think of it that way." She hugged him. "And you're not a criminal."

Helga Lietke was preparing breakfast for the two girls on Sunday morning when the phone rang. "Hello, Lietke here."

"May I speak to Klaus Lietke? This is Heinz Kluge."

Klaus came out of the bathroom and Helga handed him the phone. "Heinz Kluge," she mouthed silently.

This was a total surprise, almost a shock. "This is Klaus," he spoke into the telephone, then waited for Heinz to initiate the conversation.

They had not seen each other since Klaus had walked away from the garden shack in the spring of 1948. Heinz and Klaus, the two youngest of the Gang of Seven, had kept in touch the first year or two, and then only with an occasional phone call, until they lost all contact.

"Klaus? It's been years! How are you? I finally found your number. Who was that lovely voice answering the phone?"

After they caught up on the ten years that had elapsed—Heinz was preparing for his doctorate as a research chemist at Bayer Pharmaceutical—the subject of course turned to Gerd Schenker.

"He was your friend, Heinz, not mine. I don't want anything to do with this."

"He was nobody's friend, Klaus. Just so you know: we have no knowledge of anything, in case they should come around and ask questions. All right? We all have to say the same thing."

"Sure. What could I possibly say? I hardly know the man. I barely knew him then, and that's more than ten years ago."

"All right, so you know."

"No, I don't. And Heinz, don't call me with this stuff. I live a quiet life with my family and I want to keep it that way."

Klaus had not been very friendly with his response. He knew that, but ripping open the past was painful for him. From an unhappy childhood he went into the Hitler Youth and then the *Volkssturm*. As he hid in the rubble in Berlin at the end of the war, a Russian soldier found him and took him prisoner. With Hans-Peter and Manfred he escaped. The three years in Schlutup were not exactly happy times, except for the camaraderie. Until then he had never felt the closeness of family. That changed when Gerd Schenker came into the picture and Klaus became increasingly uneasy about the Gang's activities. Then that with Hans-Peter happened. Now a phone call brought it all back.

"What was that all about, Klaus? It's about that Gerd Schenker, right?"

"No, Helga. It's my whole past. I have really never been happy before I met you."

***

Gerd Schenker had established himself as Günter Neumann in the beautiful city of Montevideo, capital of Uruguay. He could easily lose himself in the almost entirely European population. The large community of German speaking immigrants had formed several clubs and associations. Günter Neumann carried a German passport, issued in New Zealand; it was not so easy for him to avoid joining one or another of the German *Vereins*. Excessive reluctance could be interpreted as antisocial or as having something to hide.

He disliked the group closest to the embassy. They were the snobs, looking down on all the other compatriots. *La Asociación del Cementerio Alemán*, the German Cemetery Association, fought the hardest to recruit him as a member; they needed the money. *El Club Alemán*, simply the German Club, was the most obscure. The name indicated no agenda or specific purpose for its existence. Günter had the suspicion that a considerable number of former Nazis had found refuge in El Club. He himself a fugitive from the law, did not want to socialize with them.

He could not remain anonymous for long in the German community and he could not risk being talked about as an oddball or as nonconforming, could not afford calling attention to himself. He determined it would be best to join some group and he chose the German Soccer Club, *El Club de Futbol Alemán*. Of course, he did not play; he just became a paying member, attended meetings and gatherings.

Günter transferred a substantial amount of money from Switzerland to *El Banco Central* in Uruguay and invested heavily in the winery *Bodega Juanteco Sociedad Anónima* that produced an excellent sparkling wine. Just thirty-one years old, he served on the board of directors and became a respected member of society in the capital city of Montevideo. He was beyond reproach.

After two years in Uruguay, he married the daughter of the principal shareholder and CEO of the winery, and became a citizen of Uruguay.

The arrest of several suspects in connection with the murder of Heather Lynngrave, the stylishly dressed young woman, had led Scotland Yard to discover that her murder, the diamond heist and the murder of two men in Germany were connected. Every lead, every clue, hinted at one person: the mastermind, the master criminal, Gerd Schenker—and he was missing.

The investigation had concluded that two gentlemen with credentials as dealers from Berlin had used a concentrated form of chloral hydrate to temporarily incapacitate two guards and a diamond merchant in his Johannesburg office and got away with gems estimated to be worth two million pound sterling. Those two gentlemen were found six months later shot to death, one in Berlin, the other at Helmstedt, the checkpoint at the border with East Germany.

In 1961, when the case was almost two years old and the trail became colder with each passing day, a coincidence helped bring new fuel to the stagnant investigation. The Simon Wiesenthal Organization, and several others, were deeply involved in the pursuit of Nazi criminals and followed every possible lead to locate and apprehend Adolf Eichmann, Klaus Barbie, the infamous doctor Mengele and many others. Some were thought to have escaped to Argentina, Brazil, Paraguay and Uruguay. With changed identities and, in some cases appearances, and with uncooperative Latin American authorities, these war criminals enjoyed peaceful lives until their capture decades later.

A clerk in the immigration office at the port of Montevideo, a second-generation Jewish immigrant, dedicated himself to study those who came to Uruguay to find sanctuary for political or humanitarian reasons, especially immigrants from post-war Germany. He discovered that in October of 1959, a New Zealand freighter from Wellington had arrived in Montevideo via Papeete, French Polynesia. Among the few passengers on board was a young German. His passport identified him as Günter Neumann, student, born in Munich in 1932, with resident status in New Zealand.

Barely thirteen years old at the end of the war, this young man could not have been a Nazi criminal, but the ambitious immigration clerk became curious when he read in the social column of *El Diario* that a Günter Neumann had married the daughter of the CEO of the winery *Bodega Juanteco S.A.* With hardly any difficulty he discovered that Neumann's passport and immigration papers were false, that he was almost four years older than what the documents indicated and that he had resided in New Zealand for no more than a week.

The clerk passed his findings on to his superiors at Immigration. Latin bureaucracy, moving in slow motion, compiled data on Günter Neumann and informed the local police. The chief of the metropolitan police, seeing an opportunity to further his career, found the information important enough to notify the German embassy.

The case, forwarded to headquarters of the Berlin criminal police department, landed on the desk of a young inspector who took the investigation into the identity of Günter Neumann seriously. He remembered the bizarre case of the diamond theft, and the murders connected with it, that grew cold with the disappearance of the alleged mastermind. On not more than a hunch, he located the file of the unsolved crime of the year 1959. Checking the timeline, connecting the dots, filling in the blanks, it quickly became clear to him, beyond any doubt: Günter Neumann was Gerd Schenker.

As a respected member of the higher society of Montevideo, the son-in-law of the CEO of *Bodega Juanteco*, Günter Neumann enjoyed the protection of influential citizens and political officials. It took lengthy negotiations, fighting red tape and corruption for Interpol to succeed in the extradition procedure.

Gerd Schenker, aka Günter Neumann, arrived in the summer of 1962 in Bremen, Germany, on a vessel of the Norddeutscher Lloyd. From there he was transported in handcuffs to Berlin.

***

Herr Timm reached an agreement with *Schlachtermeister* Ulrich Bolt. In 1963, Ulli was to take over the management of the business, paying Teodor Timm ten thousand marks yearly for a term of ten years. Profits above that amount were to be divided between the owner and the manager. After ten years, Ulrich Bolt would become the sole proprietor of Timm's Butchery.

Ulli asked his friend and mentor Kurt Lansen to be his accountant. With a teacher's salary at the local trade school, Kurt gladly accepted the offer and the additional income that came with it.

Heinz Kluge, research scientist at the prestigious Bayer concern in Leverkusen near Cologne, was disappointed that Klaus Lietke had ended their phone conversation on an unfriendly note. Heinz recalled the conversation months later when he wanted to bring the old Gang of Seven together for a reunion. "Don't call me with that stuff about Gerd Schenker. He was your friend, not mine," Klaus had told him.

Heinz decided to approach Kurt Lansen, whom he always still remembered as Schwarzer. He had received the announcement of Kurt and Ilse's wedding and noted their address and phone number in his notebook. He had to remind himself to call him by his real name.

"Hey Kurt, it's been a long time. How's married life? I meant to give you and Ilse a call, to congratulate you, but you know how it is... Always something..."

"Good to hear from you," Kurt answered, always the courteous one. "To what do I owe the honor?"

Heinz told him of his idea for a reunion. "I am thinking of holding it in Schlutup. You, Karl, Manfred and Kurzer—eh, I mean Ulli... You are still there. I haven't seen the place for... wait a minute. Can't be fifteen years?"

"Almost, Heinz. We aren't young kids anymore."

Then they talked for a while about their lives and their jobs, their positions in society and about the rest of the old Gang.

"Klaus Lietke..." Heinz said hesitatingly, "I don't think Klaus would like to come, unless you can persuade him. And what about Hans-Peter? You think those two have put the past behind them?"

"I'll talk to Karl and Manfred about that. Give me Klaus' phone number. I'll see what I can do." Then he added, "Manfred can give his friend Hans-Peter a call."

They avoided the subject of Gerd Schenker; Heinz did not want to give the impression that his plan for a reunion had anything to do with the upcoming trial, and Kurt wasn't sure how Heinz felt about the indictment of his former friend.

The trial of Gerd Schenker, to be held in Berlin, was scheduled for November of 1963. Witnesses were subpoenaed from as far away as South Africa, England, Switzerland and Uruguay. Schenker, formally charged with three counts of homicide and involvement in grand larceny, was held in a maximum-security prison; given his record of escaping the law, he was considered a flight risk.

Kurt Lansen discussed the prospect of a reunion with Karl and Manfred. "I like Heinz' idea. Can you imagine him as a thirty-three, thirty-four year old?"

"I can't believe I am thirty-seven!" Manfred feigned surprise. "Karl, you're the veteran among us. Forty-what... two, three?"

"I'm almost forty-four. Kurt, you're not far behind me, right?"

"Me? I was just forty-one last month. But yeah, we're no kids anymore."

"Klaus and Heinz are the youngest, both in their early thirties, I guess. I wonder what they look like today." Karl mused. "Would be fun, all of us... Doctor Heinz Kluge... Manfred, you a rich industrialist and candidate for mayor... *Schlachtermeister* Bolt..."

"You an honorable city councilman." Manfred continued the thought. "And you," he nodded toward Kurt, "a respected teacher."

"And what about Klaus, huh?" Kurt was proud of his young friend. "I understand he manages several stores in Hannover."

They were aware nobody mentioned Hans-Peter. Manfred hesitated for a moment. "Hans-Peter made sergeant in the armored division of his unit." He spoke a little too fervently, but tried to make it sound casual.

Then, after a pause, Karl brought up the subject of Gerd Schenker. "You think that's why Heinz is calling for this reunion? Right before the trial? Maybe he knows something we don't know."

"I don't think that has anything to do with it." Ulli Bolt, who had joined them, shook his head. "We shouldn't be concerned at all. They would have subpoenaed us by now."

"I agree," said Manfred. "After all, what do we really have to do with the *Diamanten Diebstahl* in South Africa and the murders that took place in 1959? We aren't even sure that Gerd is involved. I mean, that's what the trial is about, right?"

"Oh, he's involved all right," both Karl and Kurt assured him at the same time.

"Yeah, but theoretically speaking…" Manfred insisted.

They agreed that if questioned, they would deny all wrongdoing. "We can say, yes, we have at one time in the past known the man, but we know nothing about his activities."

"No," said Ulli. "I wouldn't even admit that. What? Who? I don't know what you are talking about. That's what I would say."

They came together for the reunion on the last weekend of October. Heinz arrived a day early. He had booked a room for himself and one for the Lietke family at the *Hotel Zum Anker*.

Klaus took the weekend off and drove with Helga and their two girls to Schlutup. The involvement with their former associate, their partner in the survival game of the post war years, still stirred his conscience, while Sergeant Hauser had no such qualms. "Those were just juvenile pranks," he told Manfred who was excited to have his old pal Hans-Peter as guest in his spacious home.

Manfred Scholte had reserved the large conference room at the *Hotel Zum Anker* for Saturday night. They sat down for a sumptuous dinner of several courses in a festive atmosphere. Ulli Bolt introduced Angela, a pretty young woman, as a 'friend' whom he had met at trade school years earlier. Hans-Peter showed up in dress uniform. "Still single and no commitment," he proclaimed as lightheartedly as they remembered him.

Heinz Kluge was recently engaged. "My fiancée was unable to come with me." As an excuse he offered, "She's too busy with her thesis."

Klaus and Helga had their two girls seated between them, and Hans-Peter was as far away from them as possible, at opposite ends of the table. They had greeted each other with a handshake, but exchanged no words.

The conversation all around was animated, with so many subjects to cover. The fifteen years were loaded with stories. Wine loosened their tongues; anecdotes and memories, jokes and laughter filled the room.

Klaus and Helga excused themselves early to take their girls to bed. They did not rejoin the boisterous celebration. Karl, who was not used to drinking more than a beer or two, did not participate in the alcohol-induced hilarity, but he was not a spoilsport and enjoyed being among his old friends. Krista and Frieda easily made friends with Angela, while Ilse Lansen enjoyed the attentions Hans-Peter lavished on her. She was the most sophisticated among the young women and Hans-Peter's crude compliments amused her.

The later the hour, the less chance there was to move to the subject of Gerd Schenker. Heinz had tried a couple of times to bring the conversation around to the trial that was to begin a week later, but his attempts could not compete with the topics of a lighter nature.

They celebrated into the early morning hours. Before calling it a night, Heinz announced, "We meet here for brunch at eleven o'clock. Okay? My treat."

Don't you want to make friends with Hans-Peter? You know, it's been so long..." Helga tucked the girls in and prepared to go to bed.

Klaus hung his jacket over the back of a chair and loosened his tie. "Helga, I just don't like him. With him, everything is a joke. Even that uniform fails to give him some dignity. I think the others tolerate him for old time's sake. Manfred is his only friend, and that just out of loyalty. Manfred's okay and I really like Karl and Schwarzer, I mean Kurt."

"Heinz Kluge was nice to you. I thought he would be arrogant, you know... Doctor Kluge and all... and you were a little abrupt with him when he called you, remember?"

"Yeah... Doctor Kluge. I just don't know how to talk to people with a title. But I'm not gonna let him pay for our room. Who does he think he is?" Klaus continued to undress. "I can't believe how fat he got; he must be fifty pounds overweight. I like Ulli Bolt, we have the most in common. He said Angela was just a friend. She's nice, good-looking and smart. You think she might be right for him?"

"I hope so. I liked her, too. I had a good time. Didn't you have a good time? You looked like you had a good time." Then she added, "and nobody even talked about that Gerd Schenker."

"I had an okay time. Heinz brought it up with Karl and Kurt, but then they were sidetracked. Anyway, I am glad you met all of them." He slid under the covers. "We leave right after brunch tomorrow. Okay with you?"

"Sure, if you think so. But we don't have to rush." Helga snuggled close to him. "It's only a three-hour drive."

The children were already asleep.

Klaus and Helga awoke early. The girls were having a pillow fight and their laughter rang through the room. "We are hungry! We are hungry!" they called out.

The four of them were the only guests so early on a Sunday morning, having breakfast in the big dining room. "I want to show you the town," said Klaus. "Not the outskirts; it's all new around here. You should see the woods and have a look across the border. I went only a couple of times with them, at the beginning. I told you about that. Then we can go into the garden colony, where we housed for three years."

The sky was overcast and they bundled up against a chill breeze as they stepped out of the hotel. Klaus led them to the edge of town and into the woods.

"Over there is the Wesloer Moor, the spooky place I told you about. *Die Ost Zone.*"

"Isn't it dangerous to go so close?" Helga held on to Klaus' sleeve. "Girls, take your father's hand." They felt the excitement Klaus must have felt so many years before.

"No. We stay well this side of the ditch. This is where we gathered our firewood and here is the path that leads to the crossing point."

"Let's go back. I am scared." Helga clutched her husband's arm.

"Yes, we're scared. We want to go back!" The girls huddled close to their father.

They turned around and walked to the garden colony ten, fifteen minutes away. "I don't want to meet the owners," said Klaus. " I hope they're not there."

The weather turned colder and the sky was lead gray. The colony was deserted. "Here it is. Can you believe it? Seven of us—the Gang of Seven..." They could not look in; the window was boarded up for the winter. "Looks just the way it was then." He turned around. "Let's go. I saw enough." He shuddered, from the cold or from the memory.

"How far is it to the fish factory? You told us about that. What an adventure!"

"Yes, yes! We want to see the fish factory!" repeated the girls.

"Now, you know," their mother reminded them. "Your father had to eat. There was no food in those days. That wasn't anything bad what he did."

"I know. He would have died if he hadn't stolen all that fish," said the older one.

"Then we wouldn't have had a father," her sister said gravely.

As they stood near the old piers at the fish cannery, a cold drizzle began to fall that reminded Klaus of the cold night they had brought home the twenty-two cans of herring.

On their way back to the hotel Klaus walked with them past the railroad station, which was completely renovated and did not resemble the old terminal. "You can't see the far siding from here. See that apartment building? That's where the lumberyard used to be." He hurried them on. "They'll be waiting for us with brunch." Then, as if without any importance, "This is where I confronted Hans-Peter and Gudrun. Come on, the weather is getting worse."

They arrived back at the hotel and Klaus, who did not want to give Heinz the chance to settle his hotel bill, went straight to cashier's office.

"Your room is on doctor Kluge's tab, Herr Lietke."

"Well, no. I pay for the room. Please, make the invoice out in my name."

He paid the bill, and with his family joined the group that assembled punctually at eleven o'clock in the dining room. Waiters rolled in carts with dishes of hot and cold food, pitchers of beer, and there was champagne and orange juice to prepare mimosas. The brunch was buffet-style and the guests helped themselves.

When they were all seated, Heinz Kluge tapped lightly the glass in front of him. He lifted his bulk from his chair and began to speak.

"Over fifteen years ago, we parted and went our separate ways. We were uncertain about the future. And here we are today. We survived—and not only that, we survived successfully. Every one of us has reached a status higher than we had thought possible fifteen years ago."

Murmurs of agreement, nodding and some applause interrupted his speech. Glasses were raised.

Heinz continued. "In a few days, a trial will begin in Berlin, a trial that, I am sure, all of us will follow with great interest, even with some apprehension. It is unfortunate that somehow, in a very distant way, we are linked to the man on trial. We cannot deny that. Not to the crimes he is accused of," he hastened to add, "but to the man."

Ulli Bolt raised his voice. "I don't know what you're talking about. I have nothing to do with what you are saying."

Kurt Lansen spoke calmly in the silence that followed Ulli's remark. "Heinz, we once knew the man you are talking about. That's all. That he later turned into a criminal, allegedly, I should say, has nothing to do with us. Why don't we leave that chapter of the past alone?"

"Yes, let's eat and drink and be merry," Hans-Peter intoned cheerfully. "I do not intend to let that bother me. *Prost!*" He lifted his stein to his lips and drank.

Heinz wanted to say something, but Klaus stood up and addressed him. "Is that why you asked us to come here? If you have a bad conscience, don't pass it on to us." He nudged his wife slightly. "Let's go. I didn't come here to be reminded of... of that," and turning back to Heinz, "He was your friend, remember? Not mine."

"No Klaus," Helga whispered close to him. "Don't end it like this. Sit down. Please. It's all right. I understand."

Reluctantly he sat down and said no more. A general unrest followed the awkward moment. Several voices rose at the same time. Heinz took his seat.

Karl, the oldest among them and still respected as their former leader, tried to restore the light atmosphere they enjoyed before Heinz' speech was cut short. He stood up and raised a hand.

"Please. One moment, please." Relative calm restored, Karl spoke. "Thank you, Heinz, for the great idea of bringing us together here today. I just want to say, you are right, we survived the bad times because we stuck it out together. And we all made something of our lives." After a prolonged pause he picked up his glass. "That's all," he said. *"Prost!"*

They drank and turned to the food that had remained on their plates and went over to the trays for seconds. Slowly the conversation started up again; however, the mood did not return to what it was before.

There was much backslapping. They made solemn promises not to let another fifteen years go by. The women assured one another they were glad to have met. Krista and Frieda paid special attention to Helga's two daughters.

Klaus and Heinz met on the upper floor as both of them went to retrieve the baggage from their rooms.

Heinz set his suitcase down. "Klaus, let me just say I understand your reaction. You have a lovely family and you don't want to reconnect with the past."

"Forget it. I shouldn't have reacted like that." Klaus held out his hand and Heinz took it. "You think we could be called to testify?"

"Not you. But I have been subpoenaed—as witness for the defense."

Heinz had known of Gerd Schenker's shady character when he brought him to meet Schwarzer and the Gang. Of course, what he did not know, was that one day it would come back to haunt him. Nobody could have foreseen what happened later.

One thought went round and round in his head as he sat heavily in his first class compartment on the train back to Cologne. *Where would they have been without Gerd Schenker? Through him we all had a head start when the old Reichsmark became obsolete. I made that possible, and now they don't want to be reminded of it.*

***

The trial of Gerd Schenker began on the first Tuesday in November. His lawyers went immediately on the defensive and declared, their client was innocent of all charges and should be released at once. "He has never been in South Africa and had nothing to do with the theft of the diamonds. When six months later Bernard Blum was shot in Berlin and Paul Seltzki at the Helmstedt checkpoint, he was in Frankfurt."

The judge denied his request.

The defense team easily answered the judge's questions about the one point two million pounds Sterling, deposited in Schenker's name in a Swiss bank account. "Our client had sold some commercial property to a syndicate in London. The proceeds were to fund a recreational real estate development, in which Blum, Seltzki and Schenker were partners. Herr Schenker held the check, while Blum and Seltzki took care of another transaction in Berlin. On their return, the three of them were to travel to Zurich and put the money into a corporate account, but, of course, that did not happen because Blum and Seltzki were brutally murdered, presumably by rivals. That case, still unsolved, should be pursued, instead of blaming the heinous crime on our client who had no motive at all to kill his business partners."

To the question of Schenker's hasty departure from Germany under several aliases, one of his attorneys replied, "After the mafia-style murders of Blum and Seltzki, your Honor, would you stick around and wait for the next bullet to hit you in the neck?"

On the second day of the trial, the prosecution presented its case. "Although not personally present, Schenker was the mastermind behind the diamond robbery in South Africa. We will introduce witnesses to the fact that he held a meeting with Blum and Seltzki at Frankfurt Rhein-Main airport before the two men boarded the flight for Johannesburg where the following day the robbery occurred."

The prosecutor continued with his opening statement. "We will demonstrate that six months later Gerd Schenker paid two assassins to get rid of Blum and Seltzki when they demanded their share of the proceeds. There was no real estate deal, your Honor."

Asked how the diamonds turned up in a warehouse in Hull,

England, the attorney for the prosecution explained. "The exchange took place in Frankfurt, your Honor. A stylishly dressed young woman, later identified as Heather Lynngrave, handed the accused a check for one point two million pounds Sterling and transported the loot to London. Your Honor, we will prove that the accused, Gerd Schenker, ordered the ruthless murder of Heather Lynngrave in order to recover the diamonds, a crime for which Herr Schenker will have to answer in England. Scotland Yard was able to track down and arrest the assassin in a storehouse in the port city of Hull before the diamonds could be shipped back to Germany."

And so ended day two of the trial.

During the following week and a half, the court heard witnesses for the prosecution.

Schenker's extradition to South Africa depended on the outcome of the trial in Berlin. If his involvement in the robbery could not be established, extradition was in jeopardy.

Meanwhile the two guards from Johannesburg could not describe the robbers. "We saw them only for a moment before we passed out," they declared. The merchant was also unable to describe them.

The bartender at the airport lounge, where Schenker had met with Blum and Seltzki, identified the two men from photographs. "It's them. I am sure it's them. As for the accused... I am almost certain."

The waiter from the café at Frankfurt's *Hauptwache* pointed to Gerd Schenker. "Yes, I recognize him." He could also identify from photos the two other gentlemen as Blum and Seltzki, and the stylishly dressed young woman as Heather Lynngrave.

"I remember the day Herr Schenker came into my office," said the banker from Zurich. "It was my first day as New Accounts manager and I was very nervous handling such a large amount."

Asked whether the accused said what the money was for, he answered, "If I remember correctly, he said his organization sold property in England to finance a resort to be built in Davos in the Swiss Alps."

Next were the witnesses from Montevideo: the immigration clerk who had discovered that the papers Günter Neumann presented were false, and a bank employee of *El Banco Central*, who at the time had no suspicion about Señor Neumann. The chief of the police department that arrested Günter Neumann testified self-importantly through a translator, "We had an eye on him for some time, but he never gave us a reason to question him until Interpol contacted us."

Then the prosecutor signaled the court attendant to call for the two *Bobbies* in London police uniforms. They came in with the man they had brought from England.

"Your Honor, we summoned the suspect in the murder of Heather Lynngrave, who was apprehended in Hull," and he proceeded to ask the man through an interpreter if he recognized the accused.

"That's 'im, in the gray suit, sittin' over there. One thousand pounds 'e promised me to off the female and bring 'im the stones."

The lead defense attorney jumped up. "Your Honor, what is the relevance to the case before this court? This is highly irregular. I need a word with my client."

The judge silenced the commotion in the courtroom. "Order!" He motioned to the prosecutor, "Please, proceed," and with a nod to the defense attorney, "You will get your chance."

The prosecutor declared, "We will show that this man had been hired by none other than the accused, Herr Gerd Schenker."

Last was the young inspector from Berlin police headquarters who made the positive identification of Günter Neumann as Gerd Schenker. "He did not deny his true identity and cooperated from the start."

On Monday morning of the third week, the lawyers for Gerd Schenker discredited all testimonies heard from the witnesses in the weeks before. Thereafter the presiding judge questioned the witnesses, as is the procedure in a German court of law, and none of them produced convincing evidence of Schenker's guilt in the murders of Bernard Blum and Paul Seltzki.

Although hearsay is admissible under certain circumstances,

most of the testimonies were mere speculation. Yes, the bartender at the airport lounge said he was sure of having seen the accused with the two gentlemen on the day in question; when shown the photos he recognized them as Blum and Seltzki. Yes, the waiter at the *Hauptwache* café had seen him with the two gentlemen he identified from the photos as Blum and Seltzki. He also confirmed that a stylishly dressed young woman had met with them there. Yes, the banker at the Zurich bank remembered him. And yes, the immigration clerk and the chief of police from Montevideo, as well as the inspector from Berlin police headquarters answered the judge's questions for the identity of Günter Neumann as Gerd Schenker in the affirmative.

But none of those testimonies led the judges to the conclusion that Schenker had murdered, or ordered the murders of the two victims.

As for the London cockney, all three judges agreed that the man could not be trusted. With a long list of prior convictions, and life in prison awaiting him for the murder of Heather Lynngrave, he would swear to anything in exchange for a milder sentence. Besides, if any connection with Gerd Schenker could be established, that case would come under the jurisdiction of the British courts.

The presiding judge dismissed the testimony of the two guards and the merchant from Johannesburg as irrelevant. Those witnesses had no idea who the person on trial was.

Then the day came when the judge asked to hear from Herr Schenker directly. Well attired in a blue suit, white shirt and gray tie, the defendant stepped forward, bowed respectfully, took his seat on the witness stand and acknowledged that he was under oath.

"We are most curious about the origin of the one point two million pound Sterling, which you deposited in an account at the Zurich bank. Will you, please, explain that to us," the presiding judge opened his questioning.

"Certainly, your Honor. My English grandmother, on my mother's side, had left me a property, which I sold. Miss Lynngrave, deceased under deplorable circumstances, acted as courier for the broker who facilitated the sale, and brought me the check."

"What was the role Bernard Blum and Paul Seltzki played in that transaction?"

"None, your Honor. The two gentlemen were friends of mine and we were discussing plans for a future business venture at the *Hauptwache*, a convenient meeting place in Frankfurt, where Miss Lynngrave delivered the check to me."

"Herr Schenker, I remind you that you are under oath. Your answers can have the gravest consequences. Consider well before you answer the next questions. What are the circumstances that led to the deaths of Bernard Blum and Paul Seltzki?"

"I have no idea, your Honor."

"They are the prime suspects in the diamond theft in Johannesburg six months prior to their demise and they have been seen with you at the airport lounge before they boarded the flight to Johannesburg."

"Yes, your Honor. As I said before, they were friends of mine."

"What did they tell you was their purpose of the trip to South Africa, if you recall?"

"I do not recall, your Honor."

"I repeat, you are under oath, Herr Schenker."

"I am fully aware of that, your Honor."

"What do you know about the diamond theft, Herr Schenker?"

"Absolutely nothing."

"Have you met with Herr Blum and Herr Seltzki after their return from South Africa?"

"Yes, your Honor, at the café at the *Hauptwache* in Frankfurt."

"That was six months later. Have you met with them at any other time after their return from Johannesburg?"

"Probably. Not that I recall."

"How did the diamonds, stolen six months earlier in Johannesburg, end up in Miss Lynngrave's possession, Herr Schenker? Precisely the same day she delivered a check for one point two million pounds to you in the presence of Herr Blum and Herr Seltzki?"

"I had no knowledge that Miss Lynngrave carried diamonds, nor do I know when, where or how she might have acquired them."

"What was the purpose of your meeting at the *Hauptwache*?"

"It is a convenient place, your Honor, often used for meetings because of the central location. As I said, I had arranged to meet there with my friends and partners to discuss business, and asked for Miss Lynngrave to meet me there as well."

"Was Miss Lynngrave also a partner in those discussions?"

"No, your Honor, she was not."

"How and when did you hear of the murder of your friends, eh… and partners?"

"Either on the television or the radio, your Honor. I do not remember when I first heard about it. Perhaps the same day it happened. It was a shock, as you can imagine."

"I will now ask you about your hasty departure from Germany under a false name and passport. How do you explain that, Herr Schenker?"

"My attorney has already explained that to you, your Honor. After I heard of the mafia-style execution of my friends, it was only reasonable for me to assume that I could be next. We had a plan for a very lucrative enterprise, your Honor, and it was no surprise to me that there might have been rivals. I deposited the check in a bank in Zurich and did not return to Germany."

"Why did you continue to travel under an assumed name, once you had already left the country?"

"I did not want to be mistaken for Bruno Schenker, the notorious Nazi guard from the concentration camp Theresienstadt, who is thought to have escaped to South America."

After listening to the testimonies of the witnesses and the accused, the presiding judge declared, "We are primarily concerned with the homicide of the two individuals, Bernard Blum and Paul Seltzki. The purpose of these proceedings is to establish the guilt or innocence of the person brought before us, Herr Gerd Schenker. We have so far not come any closer to his direct or indirect involvement in those murders."

The judge's remarks were addressed to the prosecuting attorney, who found himself in the uncomfortable position to respond.

"Your Honor, the suspects of having committed the atrocious acts of killing Blum and Seltzki by gunshots to the neck, have since escaped into East Germany. At the present stage of relations with the *Deutsche Demokratische Republik* and the tension between East and West, it is uncertain if they can be found and extra-dited."

After this last statement, the judges adjourned the proceedings and retired to chambers. Resuming in the afternoon, the presiding judge declared, "The political stalemate would be seriously exacerbated and could be thrown off balance if we insisted on cooperation of the *DDR* authorities. At this delicate instance of the Cold War, unforeseeable consequences could result." He paused. "We don't want to become the spark to ignite World War Three. We will pronounce judgment after considerations of the evidence brought before this court and reconvene on Tuesday of next week. This court is adjourned."

Doctor Heinz Kluge, while waiting to be called to the stand, was under extreme stress. The defense lawyers had prepared him. "We might call you as a character witness. You just have to truthfully state that you knew the defendant since your high school days, that you knew him as an honest, law abiding individual, incapable of wrongdoing or harming anyone."

Heinz had complied with the summons and a sigh of relief escaped him when his testimony was not required. He returned home, enjoyed the train ride intensely and for the first time in weeks he felt free from a burden that had oppressed him. Breathing easier, he saw the landscape passing outside the speeding train, the trees bare of leaves in the approaching winter, the fields deserted, crops harvested and meadows left to rest for a new spring that would certainly come.

Yet, some small portion of his conscience was not completely at ease. At first he did not know what bothered him deep inside and he did not want to explore it, but it worked itself to the surface. *I am relieved only because I didn't have to say in court something I am not convinced of. But I know, I know—I know… I feel it. I know he is evil. I was always scared of him. I know what he is capable of. I know. I don't want to know, but I know. I know he is guilty. I know he is guilty. I know he is.*

***

The trial of Gerd Schenker was not televised, but it received moderate coverage in the papers.

Hans-Peter, back at his unit in Bavaria, bragged about how he once knew the man accused of murder. Manfred Scholte and Karl Berger, mindful of their political careers, paid close attention to the trial, but kept their former association with Schenker to themselves. Ulli Bolt avoided the subject altogether, and Kurt Lansen emphatically refused to talk about the murder and the trial, even at home with his wife.

Klaus justified his outburst at the reunion. "Helga, I know you don't agree with me, but I am glad I stopped Heinz. The whole idea with that reunion was because he wanted to find out how we felt about that trial. He was worried. He wanted to know where we stood without telling us that he had already been subpoenaed. He wanted us to help him make up his mind how to respond in court."

"I know. It was just that it ruined the party, Klaus. We were having such a good time." Then she added, "You didn't tell anybody about his subpoena, no?"

"I didn't talk to anybody after I met him upstairs. And Helga, I didn't ruin the party. He did. He shouldn't have made that speech. He shouldn't have called for the reunion under false pretense. The others will never know he had been called to testify, unless he tells them himself."

Once more Gerd Schenker stood in front of the three-judge panel. The long months in jail before and during the trial showed in his ashen face, but his composure remained dignified, respectful and humble.

The statement of the presiding judge was short. "We have examined the evidence presented in the case against Herr Gerd Schenker. From what we have heard, we cannot arrive at a guilty verdict in the murders of Bernard Blum and Paul Seltzki. We also cannot declare the defendant innocent. For lack of conclusive evidence, Herr Gerd Schenker can only be pronounced not guilty in the murders of Blum and Seltzki; however, we reserve prejudice."

Clamor arose in the courtroom. When the tumultuous noise subsided, the judge continued. "In the matter of fleeing from justice and avoiding arrest by hiding in a foreign country, and the use of a false passport under an assumed name, this court imposes a six month suspended jail term already served, and a penalty of one hundred thousand marks. Herr Schenker, your passport remains revoked and no new passport will be granted indefinitely, on the discretion of this court. You are prohibited from leaving the country."

Gerd Schenker nodded imperceptibly; his expression remained humble and respectful.

"Under the stated provisions, Herr Gerd Schenker is to be released immediately. He is free to go." Less formally, the judge added, "One warning, Herr Schenker: in the case of murder, German law does not exclude a new trial in the event that fresh evidence warrants it. This court is adjourned."

Gerd Schenker received notification that his marriage had been annulled. Since divorce was not obtainable in Uruguay, his father-in-law had secured the annulment directly from the Vatican. The Naturalization Department of his adopted country informed him that his citizenship had been rescinded and that he was barred from entering Uruguay. Although he was legally a German subject, he had lost the privilege of free movement.

He placed an order with his broker in Montevideo to sell his shares in the winery *Bodega Juanteco* and closed out his account in *El Banco Central*. His assets dwindled under the manipulations of his agent and he was in no position to do anything about it. Yet, accumulating the remaining funds in an account at Deutsche Bank, after paying the imposed penalty of one hundred thousand marks, he was not exactly a poor man. He rented a modest apartment in Frankfurt, in the neighborhood where he grew up.

***

Wolfgang Johannsen had not doubted his decision when he defected in 1947 and walked into the *Stasi* offices in East Berlin. He was convinced it was the right thing to do. He had studied Marxism, and the ideal of Communism made sense to him. After five years at KGB headquarters in Berlin and learning Russian, he applied for transfer to Moscow.

Deep in the Soviet Union, millions of prisoners suffered from the harshest conditions in forced labor camps. Political dissidents, but also Japanese and German prisoners of war, as well as common criminals, were banished to Siberian Gulags.

Wolfgang, known as comrade Johannowich at the Politburo, went through stacks of papers that came in from the various Gulags. German being his native language, his job included listing deceased prisoners with German names, and separate political detainees from POWs and common criminals. There were also Japanese, Chinese and Korean comrades engaged in the tedious job of listing their dead compatriots.

The Gulag north of Lake Baikal was one of the deadliest. During the winter months the temperature hovered around forty degrees Fahrenheit below zero, and in the summers the mercury often climbed above one hundred. An estimated 150,000 malnourished, neglected prisoners of the Stalin era had perished during the construction of the Baikal-Amur portion of the Trans-Siberian railroad system. After Stalin's death in 1953, work on the Baikal-Amur Mainline, BAM for short, came to a halt and did not resume until 1974. By then, the prison population had been reduced significantly and conditions in the Gulags had improved.

Comrade Johannowich's index finger stopped halfway down a column. There was something familiar. *Vladimir Gerstenbauer. VoPo. May 1947. Treason. 20 years labor. Dead at Baikal-Amur, Jan. 20, 1953. Cause of death: pneumonia.*

Walter Gerstenbauer, VoPo. It was all coming back to him. *Karl and his gang... I almost got involved with them. They came to me for their knapsacks. I wonder what happened to all of them. They arrested Gerstenbauer, and then Karl... Karl was released later, but Walter was sent to Siberia where he died in '53; that's twelve years ago.*

As he continued with his tedious work he thought of his parents—*do they know where I am? Do they know I am alive? Are they alive?*

The name Gerstenbauer connected him with the past for the

first time in seventeen Years. Now, at forty, he was no longer sure Bolshevik communism was what Marx had envisioned.

***

"Guten Tag, Frau Johannsen, was gibt's Neues? What's the good news today?" Ulli Bolt greeted his customer. "Half and half as usual, for the meatloaf?"

"Ach, Herr Bolt, it's my husband's seventieth birthday. I want to surprise him. Give me a nice rump steak, his favorite."

"Sure, Frau Johannsen, and give him my best wishes. Seventy, huh? I am almost thirty-seven; can hardly believe it. This is a nice cut for you. Anything else today?"

"Herr Bolt, I want to tell you something in private. You have a minute?"

Later that evening, Ulrich Bolt sat with Kurt Lansen in his little office at the rear of the butcher shop. "I can only tell you what she told me. He is back in Berlin."

"So you think, after all these years, he's coming back? What else did Frau Johannsen tell you? This is the first time in nearly eighteen years that they heard from him? But he's still with the NKVD or KGB or whatever, huh?"

"That's what she thinks, but you know, he can't really talk on the telephone."

"How did he sound? Did she say something?"

"Don't know. That's all she could tell me. Kurt, they hope... But they are afraid. What if he tries to defect?"

Frau Johannsen set the table with their fine china, which she reserved for special occasions and placed a lit candle in the center. The smaller portion of the steak she left a little longer in the pan; she didn't like it quite as rare as her husband.

"Happy birthday, dear! Help yourself to the potatoes and the cauliflower."

"I want a beer. Don't we have any beer?"

"Oh sure, right away. I want you to enjoy your birthday, dear."

She hurried to get a bottle from the refrigerator. "I hope it's not too cold."

"What's to enjoy? Wolfgang calls after eighteen years and he doesn't even remember it's my birthday. What does he call for now? I just got used to the idea that he's dead. Now it starts all over again."

He opened the bottle and poured, creating a perfect, foamy head. "What was that scumbag's name they let free last year, Scheckler or something?"

Frau Johannsen did not have an easy life with a man of such dark nature. The older he got, the more he sank into bitterness and he was only seventy. "Schenker, dear. Gerd Schenker. Yes, dear, he is a scumbag. But let us be thankful that Wolfgang is alive."

"He couldn't have called in all these years? And what's he up to anyway with those Commies? He's no son of mine." He blew the foam off the top of his glass and drank, then went back to the subject that cluttered his mind for the past year. "Yeah, Bert Schnecker, that's it. I remember him."

"Enjoy your steak, dear. Is it right? Just the way you like it?" Frau Johannsen knew her husband had never met Schenker and she knew his senility was advancing more rapidly now.

Stoically she endured ten more years by his side. He died in 1975.

***

Doctor Heinz Kluge, severely overweight and in a bad state of health had undergone several operations, but was able to resume working in the research and development department at Bayer Pharmaceutical. In 1970, however, a particular delicate surgery on his spine forced him to retire early. Suffering from chronic back pain, diabetes and near-blindness he was an invalid when he was just forty years old.

His wife Dotti left him and their two sons after years of a loveless marriage. He raised the boys with the help of a governess whom he eventually married; the sons, grown and away at universities, no longer needed her, but Heinz did, and she took over essentially as his nurse.

Disturbing news reached him one day in early 1980. Gerd Schenker, with whom he had exchanged sporadic phone calls, had been missing for three days when his body was found floating in a canal near a Frankfurt suburb. Foul play was suspected and an investigation was underway. Schenker was fifty-one years old.

Klaus Lietke, too, heard it on the evening news. "Finally, that's over. The man lived a life of crime, if you asked me. I wonder what he was involved in and who put an end to it."

"Klaus, does that mean you can now forget about that, once and for all?" Helga had endured his moodiness, his depressions, his bouts with a guilty conscience throughout the years. They had a good marriage, but from time to time one event or another created rifts between them. "Let's never even think about it ever again."

"I'll try, Helga. I think it will be easier now."

Klaus and Helga's daughters, in their mid-twenties, were both married. They had children of their own and lived near their parents in Hannover.

"We have our family to look after and to enjoy, so let's forget about everything else." She snuggled up to him. "You want to ask them over for Sunday? The little ones always are so much fun."

On a Sunday in the spring of 1980, Manfred and Kurt sat with Karl on the balcony of his home in Schlutup. There was not much of a surprise among them over the news of Gerd Schenker's death. They had distanced themselves from the time they had known him and from the later events; they took the news of his murder as a natural consequence of his lifestyle.

"Something like that had to happen, the way he lived his life," Manfred commented. "I just wonder what led to his demise and who..."

"I don't even care," Karl interrupted him. "Maybe the same ones who killed Blum and what's-his-name."

Kurt said, "That was in '59, over twenty years ago. They never caught them, huh?"

Krista came out. "Now you've got somethin' to talk about again." She shivered and went back inside. "Still too cold for me out there." Before she closed the door, she asked, "Isn't Ulli coming over today?"

"I don't know. Haven't seen him for a couple of weeks." Kurt thought for a moment. "Last time I went to look over his books he told me not to bother; said he had already made all the entries. Hm." He paused. "I found that a little strange. He never did that before; he never cared. Never wanted anything to do with the books."

"Maybe he's learning in his old age," Manfred laughed.

"He's not that old, Manfred; isn't he younger than you?"

"Yeah, that's right. But still, all these years in business? He must have learned something about keeping records. What do you think, Kurt?"

"Maybe," and reflecting on the recent years, "ever since he no longer had to make payment to Herr Timm in Denmark, he took more money out for himself. He didn't explain that to me and I didn't ask. It's his money. I just keep the books, write the paychecks for the butcher who works for him and for his apprentices, and prepare the taxes." Puzzled, he paused to think about it. "Hm. Strange. I don't know. Something isn't right. You haven't seen him either lately, huh?" He looked from Karl to Manfred.

They looked at each other. "Can't be a woman, or..." Karl wondered.

"Nooo, no way," Manfred dismissed the idea. "Last time he had a girlfriend was years ago. Angela, remember her? Nice looking, smart. Married a doctor from Hamburg."

"Then, what is it?"

"I will look into it," Kurt decided. "Something must be going on."

"To change the subject," Manfred interjected, "I heard from Hans-Peter. He's coming up next week to spend a few days here."

"Oh yeah? He finally settled down, huh? Didn't he get married?" Karl asked.

"He married a young Polish girl after his twenty-year service in the *Bundeswehr*. Now he manages a branch of the security firm

Wach und Schliessgesellschaft, in München."

"Security firm? Huh, that's the right job for him," Karl laughed.

"Oh, come on, Karl. You still see him as that crazy kid. He's gotten older too, you know." Kurt always gave everybody the benefit of the doubt. "I'll bet he's a serious, middle-aged man like the rest of us."

"Okay, maybe. Does he have any kids, Manfred?"

"I hope not. How do you think they'd turn out?" The idea of his old buddy as a father amused him. "You can ask him yourself this weekend."

Still the mayor of Schlutup, Manfred delegated the management of his chain of hardware stores into the capable hands of Richard Groth, his general manager; he himself merely served as a consultant. Most of the time he could be found at City Hall, or in the attic of his mansion where he set up a model railroad. Manfred had become a rich man.

Nineteen year-old Manfred Junior, still away in college, would take over the business. His daughter Birgit, at eighteen a stunning brunette, studied fashion design in Paris.

"We will have a mini-reunion on Saturday night at my house," Manfred announced to his friends Karl and Kurt. "I gave Ulli a call, too. He said he would come. Maybe we'll find out what kind of trouble he's in."

Hans-Peter drove into town with his sporty Fiat convertible. His wife Ninotchka, plump and bleach blonde, was outgoing, loved to laugh, but spoke little German. Manfred and Frieda welcomed them into their home. Hans-Peter still had that mischievous smile, always as if up to some prank. Nina was a perfect match. Loud and full of energy, she felt right at home. She got the party going as soon as Kurt and Ilse arrived. When Karl and Krista rang the bell, they already heard the laughter before Frieda opened the door.

Indeed, Hans-Peter had become a little more serious in his mid-fifties, but Ninotchka kept him from aging. His dark hair had grayed at the temples and thinned a little on top; a few more pounds around the midriff suited him well.

"Ulli is not coming, I guess," Frieda was saying as they sat down to dinner. At that moment the doorbell rang.

"I'll get it." Krista got up; she sat closest to the door.

"Ulli! What's the matter? Why are you...?" Krista's voice came from the hall.

Kurt put down his napkin and got up. Ulli Bolt stood in the door, disheveled, as if he had been sleeping in the street. Alcohol was on his breath.

Manfred went over to them. "Ulli! You been in an accident? Come, let me get you cleaned up. Tell me, what happened? Frieda, give me a hand. You stay where you are, enjoy your meal. We'll be right there. Sit down, Kurt. Karl, pour some wine."

Hans-Peter, who rose from his chair to greet Ulli, stopped halfway up and sat back down. They had not seen each other in nearly twenty years, since their last reunion.

Manfred and Frieda walked Ulli into the bathroom and closed the door. Kurt and Krista joined the others at the table. Ninotchka reached for her glass. "That was funny!"

Her improper remark did not help much to bring the stalled dinner party back on track, but it restored some of the light atmosphere. They passed the tureen of minestrone around, helped themselves to the garlic bread and ate while commenting on trivial topics.

Frieda came back to the table and pulled up another chair. "They'll be here in a minute. Everything is all right. He had a little to drink, that's all."

Manfred and Ulli came back from the bathroom. After a few seconds of hesitation, Hans-Peter stood up and reached out to greet his old friend. "Hey, Kurzer, I mean Ulli! What are you up to, old man? Good to see you!"

Ulli almost ignored him, but absentmindedly shook Hans-Peter's hand, then sat on the chair Manfred pulled out for him. His hair was combed, his tie straightened. He was pale and the stubble on his face was at least forty-eight hours old.

"I'm not hungry," was all he said.

"That's okay, Ulli. Take your time," Frieda said soothingly.

"Perhaps a glass of water…"

"Thanks. Kurt, can I talk to you? I mean afterwards? I really need to talk to you."

***

The housing complex near the old *Hansawerke* where Heinz Kluge used to live with his parents had been torn down in the early seventies. The aircraft parts factory itself was converted into a two-story parking garage and a modern *supermarket* occupied the site next to it. Karl Berger, on the board of urban planners at the city council, had approved the building of the *Einkaufzentrum.*

Schlachtermeister Ulrich Bolt, as a member of the Guild of Independent Store Owners, had voted against the establishment of the Supermarkt. Now the convenience of shopping for all their needs in one place gradually drew the housewives to the *Einkaufzentrum.* Although several greengrocers, fish stores and neighborhood bakeries had to close their doors, Ulli retained a core clientele because of the fine quality of his products and the specialty items he offered, such as game, fowl and fresh sausages. His business, still known as Timm's Butchery, did well and continued to flourish. No one knew this better than Kurt Lansen, his accountant.

No wonder then that it came as a shock to the community when on Monday morning after the party at Manfred Scholte's house a sign at the door to Timm's Butchery read: ***Closed until further notice.***

At the mini-reunion the evening before, when the others had moved into the living room, Ulli confessed to Kurt, that for nearly ten years he had been gambling at the Casino of nearby Neustrand, beach resort town and playground for tourists and the rich from Hamburg and Berlin.

"When Angela turned me down and married that doctor from Hamburg, I started to try my luck at the roulette table," he confided in Kurt. "It went well at first," he told him. "I was winning. I went Friday nights and sometimes during the week. When I lost money,

I usually made up for it the next time. Then I had a losing streak and I went more often in the evenings after closing shop to win back my losses." His long speech had exhausted him. "I am ruined, Kurt. I am totally ruined."

Late that night, Kurt and Ilse took Ulli to his home above the butchery. "First thing tomorrow we go to the bank, place a stop payment on all your outstanding checks, and then I take you to my friend, lawyer Sam Morgenstern," Kurt told him. "Now, go to bed. Shower and shave and be ready early. I'll pick you up around eight thirty. We will straighten this out. Good night."

Kurt and Ilse drove home. "How bad can it be?" Ilse asked her husband. "Could he really be ruined?"

"We'll see tomorrow. After the bank and the lawyer, I will check the books, his receipts and payment stubs. There must be unpaid invoices, demands from creditors, returned checks for lack of funds—things like that. Later I'll have to take an inventory."

In the morning he told Ilse, "I won't be able to come in for lunch. I have a class at eleven thirty and another at three in the afternoon. Do me a favor, call Manfred or Karl. Tell them not to talk about this until we know the whole story."

By eight in the morning, when Kurt arrived, Ulrich Bolt was downstairs in his office, rummaging through his papers.

"Let's go," Kurt hurried him on. "You can do that later."

At the bank they found that several checks had already been returned. The manager was sympathetic but firm. "Herr Bolt, you are three months behind on your loan payments. The entire balance plus interest and penalties were due on the fifteenth. We had no choice but to close your account. Under the contract, our demands are to be satisfied before all others."

Kurt answered for Ulli and asked. "How much is the deficit?"

"I will have that for you in the afternoon. There will be fees for canceled and returned checks in addition to the outstanding principal, penalties and accrued interest—all that is now due immediately." The manager added in a more conciliatory tone, "Herr Bolt, we will try to avoid criminal charges, in consideration of your standing in the community, but we will have to have your complete cooperation and honesty in this."

Again, Kurt responded. "You can be absolutely certain of Herr Bolt's sincere efforts to make the necessary arrangement. We will seek Morgenstern & Son's advice." He stood up and nudged Ulli lightly to get up, too. "Sam Morgenstern will be in touch with you this afternoon," he told the bank officer.

Returning to the store, they chose the side entrance to avoid the small crowd that had gathered in front. Once inside, Kurt asked Ulli to collect all records while he called the law office of Morgenstern & Son. "Sam, I need to talk to you right away. It's an emergency. You have to see us. Bolt and I will be there in twenty minutes. Do this for me, will you, please?"

Frau Johannsen received another phone call from her son. Since he had returned to Berlin, Wolfgang called his mother once or twice a month. The conversations were superficial chitchat; he never gave any indication of his whereabouts or the work he did. No address, no phone number, no clear answers to her questions.

His call that morning had confused her. He sounded different, in a hurry. *I'm on my way to... Can't tell you more... Next time you hear from me...two or three days... See you then...* Click, and the phone went dead.

Those fragments went round and round in her head. Oh, and *don't talk to anyone...* were his last words before he hung up.

Now, the eighty year-old woman stood in a small group of customers in front of the butcher shop, speculating on the reason for the sign on the door.

"A death in the family?"

"No, he has no one."

"He could be ill. He was very pale last time I saw him."

"This is not like him," Frau Johannsen observed as she walked away. *Where will I get a nice pot roast for Wolfgang when he comes home? "See you then..." is what he said.*

She felt the need to talk to somebody. Now she had no one.

"Sam, thanks for seeing us on such a short notice. You know Herr Bolt. We are in a bit of trouble."

Herr Morgenstern listened, looked at the papers they had

brought, asked a few questions and said, "Is this a complete list of your creditors? Forty-five thousand marks? You have assets, the house, inventory? I need all that. Now, what about the bank loan?"

Kurt answered. "There's a loan of around seventy thousand. Interest, late penalty—we will get that this afternoon. We might be looking at hundred twenty, hundred twenty-five thousand all together."

"What about the house?" The lawyer looked from Kurt to Ulli.

"I paid off the business, but the house still belongs to Timm's daughter. I haven't paid her the rent for three months,"

"How much is the rent?"

"Two hundred forty a month."

"So that's another seven hundred twenty marks. Anything else?"

"The truck. Twenty thousand, but they can take the truck. It's worth more than that."

"Might not be so easy. What else? Salaries?"

"Kurt, you paid them last week, no?"

"No. You said, you didn't need me, remember?"

"Then I owe them, I think, for one week."

"That's about five hundred marks," Kurt estimated.

"Taxes?" demanded Morgenstern as he scribbled on his legal pad.

"They are up to date," said Kurt. "I'm sure of that."

"That's a relief." Sam Morgenstern exhaled. "So. We will have to add all that up, file for insolvency with the court and send notices to the creditors." He leaned back in his leather recliner. "Then there is the question of how you got yourself into this situation. The bankruptcy law, paragraph 283, section one, provides for five years in prison and X amount penalty. That is if criminal intent can be established. Criminal intent is a) hide assets or render them useless; b) losses due to risky speculations, gambling and such; and, of course, c) altering records. In other words: cooking the books." He looked over his half-moon glasses, rocking slowly, hands folded behind his head. "Any of that the case?" He observed Kurt and Ulli as they exchanged glances. "I am your lawyer, you have to be truthful with me."

"Look, Sam." Kurt took up a conspiratorial tone of voice. "My good friend Ulrich Bolt, a solid citizen, as we all know, made some bad choices. There is no crime here, we know that, right? He had the best intentions, but—look, he got himself into a bit of gambling, playing the roulette, you know. An innocent pastime that went out of control. That's the trouble we are talking about here. An innocent pastime."

Sam Morgenstern did not change his posture, kept rocking in his chair, continued to look over the upper rim of his glasses. "Paragraph 283, section two, provides for two years in prison and a penalty of X marks, if the judge finds the cause of the insolvency to be risky or reckless actions, without criminal intent."

For a moment, there was no sound other than the tick-tock of the grandfather clock in one corner of the office. "Is that how you want to plead?" asked the lawyer.

"Sam, is there... I mean, can we... Sam, look. You know Ulrich Bolt. A good man. Prison? Can you imagine what that would do to him? Can't we get around that prison thing? What good would that do in this case?"

"Depends on the judge. First, let's get the numbers together. I will notify the state attorney and keep this list of the creditors. They have to be advised."

Kurt looked at his watch. "Damn, I'll be late for my class. I've got to run. Ulli, work with Herr Morgenstern, if he has any more questions."

"No, I don't need anything else for now," said Sam. "I'll be in touch."

Kurt just made it to school for his eleven thirty-class and Ulli Bolt arrived home somewhat relieved that his heavy burden was now in capable hands. *A shared load is half the load,* he reckoned. *If only I can stay out of prison.*

Schlutup was still a small town, with a small-town character, and rumors spread like wild fire. By late afternoon most of the population had heard of the bankruptcy of Timm's Butchery, and the following day it was in the local morning paper. ***Timm's Butchery closes its doors***. The article, however, stated it was the result of the *disregard of the city's government toward the small shop owners by allowing the establishment of yet another Supermarkt*—a smear tactic of the opposition against the mayor and the city council in the upcoming elections.

That was a lame effort, for mayor Scholte and Councilman Berger would win by a large margin. Ulrich Bolt benefited from the wrong assertion by the media, and his gambling addiction remained hidden from the general public.

The judge ruled that, in order to keep his business afloat, Herr Bolt made the foolish decision to gamble at the roulette tables of the Casino in Neustrand. The stress over the new *Einkaufzentrum* was to blame for his irrational attempt to save the business.

No prison term was handed down. The verdict came to a penalty of twenty-five thousand marks, spread over ten years, payable out of income from any future employment, and a ban on starting a new business for the next seven years.

Timm's Butchery never reopened. The bank collected the meager assets and the creditors were left without recourse. For old time's sake, Teodor Timm's daughter forgave Ulli the three months rent he owed.

The proceedings in bankruptcy court had dragged on into the summer. Unable to come up with the rent money, Ulrich had to vacate the apartment above the store. Manfred Scholte hired him as caretaker for one of his buildings, in exchange for a one-room basement apartment and a small salary, and Karl Berger used his influence to secure a part-time job for him at the meat counter of the *Einkaufzentrum*.

***

Frau Johannsen waited day after day for the arrival of her son. She had not heard from him since that phone call. *Two or three days... See you then...* he had said. Eight weeks passed without further notice from him.

Then, in the summer, something quite extraordinary happened. Wolfgang Johannsen, as a member of an East German trade commission, traveled to Gdansk, the Polish port city on the Baltic Sea.

He was able to defect and seek refuge in the house of a functionary of the illegal Underground Free Trade Union. On 14 August 1980, the Solidarity movement under Lech Walesa staged the strike at the Lenin Shipyard and Wolfgang escaped as a stow-away on a freighter to Szczecin, formerly Stettin, on the border between Poland and East Germany. There he managed to board a ferry to Malmø, Sweden. Unannounced, he arrived in Schlutup on the last day of August.

Thirty-three years lay between his disappearance in 1947 and the day he set foot in his hometown. He was fifty-six years old. Mother and son greeted each other warmly, but their embrace was almost as if they were strangers. Frail, eighty year-old Frau Johannsen was unable to shed tears of joy, thinking of her late husband. *He's no son of mine,* the feeble-minded man had said repeatedly.

Wolfgang had too much to say, he could not find the beginning, so he limited his story to the last days of his odyssey, from Gdansk via Sweden to Schlutup. A time would come to fill in the blanks, his years in Berlin with the *Stasi,* then Moscow and the KGB, and again Berlin.

But the time never came. Frau Johannsen lived only to see her son come back. She died the week after Wolfgang's return.

For Wolfgang Johannsen it was a tragic homecoming. His father had died years earlier and his mother succumbed within days to the overpowering emotion caused by his return. He found himself in a destitute situation. Since his father's death, his mother had lived on a meager pension. There were no savings and there was no life insurance. Wolfgang applied for benefits from the social assistance program and, without the prospect ever to be able to repay a loan, he was turned down. Unemployment benefits could not be calculated because he had no employment record. With money left over from the social security allowance for his mother's cremation, he went to Hamburg to apply for asylum as a political refugee. The office for repatriation could not verify his story and officials at the British embassy distanced themselves from issues of an inflammatory nature at that stage of the Cold War.

The bank repossessed the house in which his parents had lived since they were married and in which he was born. A second mortgage on the property resulted in a deficit for which Wolfgang was now liable. He had to declare bankruptcy.

Homeless and without friends, Wolfgang approached Ulrich Bolt, who less than three months earlier had lost his prosperous business to gambling.

"There's no opening here at the market right now," Ulli told him. "I work only part-time and that's temporary. In Neustrand they always need some help with the gardening. It's not much of a job, but in the evening you have a few marks for a meal."

The summer of 1980 faded into a mild autumn. Wolfgang hitchhiked to Neustrand.

Balding and pale, he no longer gave a strong and healthy impression. His gray East German suit of shabby fabric hung loosely on his middle-aged frame.

"The walks and the lawn have to be cleared of leaves," the foreman explained to him. "Paper napkins, candy wrappers, cigarette butts go in the trash cans. In the evening you take the trash to the dumpster. Got that? Today and tomorrow. After that, we'll see."

Wolfgang rested for a moment and supported himself on the long handle of his rake. Gardeners tended the grounds and flowerbeds surrounding the casino and a couple of hourly workers assisted with maintenance. He listened to the music that came from the adjacent coffee garden. Dreamy tunes were interrupted by moderate applause. A baritone, who joined the three-piece ensemble, consisting of piano, violin and cello, gave a heartfelt rendition of the Volga song. Wolfgang's eyes filled with tears.

That night he spent on the beach, scarcely sheltered by the dunes from the night breeze coming over the ocean. He had allowed himself only a bowl of soup and a cup of tea. In the evening of the second day, he hitchhiked back to Schlutup, three marks and change in his pocket.

In his hopelessness he overcame his reluctance to call on city councilman Karl Berger, former leader of the Gang, who had asked him for help with their knapsacks. *That's nearly thirty-five years ago—will they still remember? Will they want to remember? Would they even talk to me, the defector?*

"Yes, Ulli Bolt told me you came back. I really can't help you. I'm not in construction any more. Unemployment is high. Talk to Manfred Scholte. He's the mayor. Maybe he has something."

With nothing to lose, he went to City Hall. Mayor Scholte greeted him jovially. "So, you came back after all these years. No, I hold no grudge. That's all in the past. We have other things to worry about." He paused and contemplated Wolfgang's haggard appearance. "Work? A place to stay? That's difficult nowadays. You see, the prosperity is in the big cities, the industry. Hamburg, the Ruhr." Manfred made a sweeping gesture. "Schlutup? We're just hanging on, with unemployment through the roof. I've done all I could to attract business, but it's tough." He thought for a moment. "Tell you what: you know Kurt Lansen? I heard they need a custodian at his trade school. Comes with a small apartment in the basement. You know something about maintenance, the furnace, the shower rooms?"

With a flicker of hope, intent on not letting this slip away from him, some enthusiasm came into Wolfgang's voice. "Sure, I've done that kind of work in Berlin." He had been on friendly terms with one of the caretakers of the *Stasi* building, when he first arrived in East Berlin. Once he had helped with the cleaning of the huge oil furnace. "Where can I find Kurt?"

"I'll give him a call. Wait right here."

Wolfgang met Kurt Lansen in his office at the school. Kurt was doubtful of Wolfgang being right for the job, but he was willing to stick his neck out and recommend him to the board.

"The old man retires the end of the month. You would have to work with him a couple of weeks to familiarize yourself with the chores. The pay is not much. Is that okay with you?" Kurt looked at him; he really wanted to help. "I can let you know tomorrow. Where can I reach you?"

Wolfgang had slept the last few nights in the homeless shelter near the freight station and ate at the soup kitchen. "I can stop by tomorrow," he told Kurt. "I don't have an address right now, you know." He thanked Kurt. "I really need this job."

***

Three uneventful years followed. Ulrich Bolt became supervisor for the meat department and continued as caretaker in one of Manfred's buildings.

Wolfgang Johannsen, custodian at the *Handelschule*, worked diligently and kept to himself. He had no friends and socialized with no one.

As the summer of 1983 turned into autumn and the leaves in the regrowing forest of Schlutup turned a golden yellow and rich deep red, something happened that brought the original members of the Gang of Seven closer together—not in the geographical sense, but in spirit.

"How about that? Did you see that on the television just now?" Karl called Manfred moments after it was on the evening news. "About Heinz Kluge?"

"Heinz? No, I didn't have it on. What are you telling me? He's dead?"

"Took an overdose of barbiturates. 'Research scientist Heinz Kluge at Bayer Pharmaceutical', they said. That's him, right? Now they are investigating, but it seems he left a note. Couldn't take it any more. All that pain, the blindness, the diabetes and then kidney dialysis."

"Suicide. One of us. Who would have thought. And he was only in his early fifties."

"Yeah. I guess we will hear more about that. Talk to you tomorrow."

"Thanks for telling me. Good night." Manfred hung up.

Frieda asked, "What about Doctor Heinz Kluge? Suicide, you said?"

"Yeah. Killed himself. He has suffered for many years. His kids are grown up; he had nothing to live for. I guess I can't blame him, with all that misery. Don't know what I would do."

"Now don't you talk like that. Be thankful we're both healthy, and Birgit and Junior, too." She gave her husband a hug. "We will live long, happy, healthy lives."

"You think so? Wait until I trade you in for a younger model."

"Don't you dare!" She pinched him hard on the cheek.

"Ow! I mean a younger model just like you! Exactly like you—just younger."

"You couldn't handle..." She couldn't finish the sentence. His lips covered her mouth.

Klaus Lietke and Helga were holding hands, sitting on the couch watching the evening news on television. "Of the old Gang, he and I were the youngest. Actually, he was a few months younger than me. I am glad I made up with him after that reunion party, but then we never heard from him again. How long ago is that?"

"1963, October. Remember? Almost twenty years." Helga's memory was as sharp as ever. "He was already overweight. Didn't look healthy even then."

"I could never kill myself. Could you?"

"Not as long as I have you, the girls and the grandchildren." She moved closer to him, gave him a kiss on the cheek. "Let's not talk about things like that."

Hans-Peter called Manfred. "Heinz died of an overdose. Did you know he was on drugs?"

"Listen, he was not on drugs. You got it wrong. He committed suicide. He left a note saying, he did it because he couldn't take it any more. Constant pain, blind and in a wheelchair. His son's were not close to him—he had nobody. I can't blame him."

"Oh, all right. That's different. Nina told me. Her German isn't that good, you know. She mixes things up all the time. It's hilarious! She's so funny." Heinz Kluge's death did not touch him deeply. Nothing ever did. "So, what else is new? Kurzer, Ulli Bolt, doing okay now at the *Einkaufzentrum*, I hear."

"Yeah, he's the head of the meat department. He also takes care of one of my buildings."

"And that bastard, the one that defected to the Commies and came back? Johannsen?"

"Ah, he's a broken man. Talks to no one. Has a job as a school custodian. Look, he came to his senses. Give it a rest."

"All right. Say hello to Karl and Schwarzer, I mean Kurt. And Ulli, too." He hung up and turned to Ninotchka. "You told me he was on drugs."

"No. Not *on* drug. *Took* drug. I say: *took* drug. You never listen me. You no understand German?"

"There isn't even someone we can send a card to. No condolences to anybody." Kurt was talking to Ulli Bolt. They met occasionally in the evening for a glass of beer at the pub near the *Einkaufzentrum*.

"I guess his sons will at least take care of the funeral arrangements," said Ulli. "Once the medical examiner releases the body."

"I don't know where the sons live. I don't even know their names."

"Me neither." Ulli motioned to a young man who entered the pub and hesitated inside the door. When he came closer, Kurt saw his full head of blond hair was actually a toupee and that he was not as young as he seemed from a distance.

"This is Ralph Werner," Ulli blushed as he introduced him. "We are… eh, close friends. Ralph, this is Kurt Lansen. I told you about him."

Ralph almost performed a curtsy, crimson color spreading from his ears over his cheeks. "Pleased to meet you, I'm sure," he stumbled and stepped to the far side of Ulli, away from Kurt.

So, Ulli moved over to the other team on the playing field, thought Kurt and after some small talk and another glass of beer he excused himself. "Promised Ilse I'd be home by seven. Nice meeting you, Rolf."

"Likewise, I'm sure."

"It's Ralph, R-a-l-p-h," Ulli corrected.

"I am sorry, Ralph" *Hiuh, let me get out of here.* Kurt left the pub.

The following day Kurt talked to Manfred in the mayor's office. "So, you knew about that? Why didn't you say something? Have you met this R-a-l-p-h?"

"I haven't met him, but I knew. Why? Does it matter?"

"Of course not. It's just... I had no idea."

"I think it's a big step for Ulli to let you meet his companion. People are just beginning to accept *Schwule*. For most, it's a big secret. To come out and say..."

"He didn't say anything," Kurt cut him off. "'My close friend', he called him."

"Still, he knows it's obvious. He came out of his shell and I give him credit."

"You are awfully tolerant, Manfred. Since when, huh?"

"Let's just say, I have... My daughter, Birgit... She's that way. She told her mother, and Frieda, of course, told me."

Kurt was quiet for a moment. After a pause he shook his head, as if clearing his mind, and said, "Manfred, how did you take it? How does Frieda feel about it?"

"I was speechless at first. Not angry. Speechless. But, since she is still in Paris, I don't have to deal with it. Frieda doesn't seem to mind, or she keeps it to herself and we don't talk about it. Now, if it had been Junior..." A phone call interrupted their conversation. Manfred just said a few mhms and ahas, and hung up. "Where were we—yes; now, Ulli Bolt is not my son. If he were, I'd beat the crap out of him." Then he added, "With a daughter it's different, I guess."

Kurt went home. Ilse, who has always been fond of Ulli, said, "He never had any luck with the opposite sex. I am glad for him to have someone in his life. What business is it of ours." When Kurt did not reply, she asked, "are you all right?"

"Ah, what? Yeah. I'm okay." Kurt remained uncommonly quiet and distant.

*****

Ulli Bolt, who had relatives on the other side of the Iron Curtain, wondered if the frontier would ever be opened for normal travel. "Ralph says, something is happening inside the Soviet Union," he said to Kurt over a beer in the pub. "He reads all the papers and listens to all the news. He's very smart, you know."

"What does he do for a living? You don't talk much about him."

"Oh, he doesn't really work, or anything like that. He manages an art gallery in Hamburg, but he thinks of it as work. His parents were artists."

"Is he an artist, too?"

"No, he collects art and exhibits it. He has lots of money." Ulli fidgeted before he spoke again." Kurt, I am... you know... We are involved. You probably know that already. I would move in with him in Hamburg. I just don't know how to tell Manfred. You think he would be offended? He helped me a lot, you know."

"Manfred doesn't care. You know about his daughter Birgit, right? She made Paris her home and hardly ever shows up here."

Ulli motioned the waiter for another round. "We have been...eh, friends now for over three years. We really get along well. You think it would be a good idea to move in with him?"

"How would I know, Ulli. If you think so... Look at Karl and Krista. They're not married and live together for thirty years. Wouldn't that be the same thing? No, huh?" He waited for Ulli to say something. When he didn't, Kurt repeated, "No, huh?"

"Well," Ulli hesitated and then said, "It's not really the same. Society looks at us differently." He drank, then set the glass down. "I will talk to Manfred tomorrow. Ralph wants me to live with him. He has a big apartment; I've seen it."

"Do what you think is right. I can't tell you that." They both drank, then Kurt asked, "What did you mean by 'something is happening in the Soviet Union?'"

"Ralph says, now that Gorbachev became their leader, there will be changes."

Kurt knew what Ulli was talking about, but he wanted to hear more. "Ralph knows a lot about that, huh? What else does he say?" "Well, I don't understand it all, but he says Yuri Andropov promoted Gorbachev to be the leader of the Communist Party. When Andropov died, Gorbachev became General Secretary under Chernenko. Ralph talks about Perestroika and Glasnost, things like that. He says there will be big reforms."

"Yeah, that means new development and openness. Does he think there will be a reunification?

"You mean, like East and West? You must be kidding. Impossible!" They both laughed quietly and shook their heads. "If they open the border I want to go and visit my relatives," said Ulli. "I wanted to do that for a long time."

Ulrich Bolt did not apply for a permit to visit his aging aunt and uncle in East Germany, but in 1986 he moved to Hamburg. His friend Ralph Werner had struggled for some time already with a disease caused by the Human Immunodeficiency Virus, HIV. In the fall of that year his illness progressed rapidly to AIDS. He died of pneumonia four months after Ulli had moved in with him.

Even before the funeral, a brother and sister Ralph had never mentioned surprised Ulli with the request to vacate the spacious apartment he had shared for such a short time with his friend.

The will Ralph had drawn up with his attorney weeks before he died made no mention of Ulrich Bolt. Once again, Ulli was homeless.

PART THREE

During the 1960s, '70s and into the '80s, the possibility for a reunification of the two Germanys seemed unrealistic. At the ever deepening cleft between East and West the idea existed perhaps as wishful thinking in the minds of many Ossies, while the Wessies considered it with less enthusiasm. Both sides desired a German unity, but they viewed the consequences differently in East and West.

On 9 November 1989, news about the breach of the Berlin Wall spread around the globe. The movement had started in Hungary with the border opening into Austria. Then it swept over Poland and culminated in breaking down the Wall that divided the world in two opposing political, social and economic ideologies. On 18 March 1990, the first free elections since 1932 were held in the eastern part of Germany, marking the end of the *Deutsche Demokratische Republik*. By that time, over 100,000 people had crossed into West Germany.

The official reunification of the two Germanys took place on 3 October 1990.

Erich Honecker, the last Communist leader of the *Deutsche Demokratische Republik*, was tried for ordering to shoot anyone climbing the Wall. He was later released, being in poor health, and allowed to join his daughter in Chile, where he died of cancer.

CITY HALL
AND
FIREWORKS

K arl Berger handed in his resignation from the city council. For twenty-seven years he had served on the board for urban development. His seventieth birthday was coming up.

"I want to be free from all those political shenanigans that come with the job," he told his boss, the mayor. "Manfred, we've both been in it for a quarter of a century. When are you gonna quit?"

Manfred Scholte was seven years younger than Karl. Still in good health, he looked forward to his retirement, travel and pursue his hobby, the model railroad he had installed in the attic of his villa, but he said, "I think I'll stay on until I'm sixty-five, another couple of years. Frieda wants me to give it up, so I told her I won't run for another term."

Karl's plans were dashed by the earthshaking, unforeseen, most extraordinary event of the twentieth century. On his birthday, 9 November 1989, the date he had specified for his retirement, East Berliners broke through the Wall in triumphant ecstasy. In the days that followed, a flood of *Ossies* crossed the border and crowded into cities, towns and villages. Everywhere people opened their homes to their East German brethren and welcomed them with genuine warmth. Households were filled to capacity with long-missed family, friends and even strangers.

The astonishing fact was that they brought money. In the state-run East German economy, there was no unemployment. Everybody had a job, no matter how meaningless, how trivial or bureaucratic, and there were no opportunities to spend the income. They could not travel abroad; their vacations in communist party recreation centers were paid for and luxury items were not available.

The exchange rate of the East German to the West German mark was four to one, and business in Schlutup was booming. Automobile dealerships registered record sales. Families arrived in ill equipped Trabants and Wartburgs, with cash in bags, boxes and suitcases. They crowded streets and highways, polluting the air with the exhausts of gas-oil mixture fuel. They left in Mercedes, Opels and BMWs. The sale of household items, clothing, even jewelry left stores short of inventory. It was a shopping frenzy and the cash registers rang non-stop through extended business hours.

City employees, police and volunteers were on hand to regulate and direct the overpowering influx of visitors, shoppers as well as the curious, and they all were treated as guests. Manfred Scholte and his staff at City Hall worked into the evenings and on the weekend, and so did Karl Berger and Kurt Lansen. Krista, Frieda and Ilse helped out where they could.

Among the guests from the East was Ulrich Bolt, who had moved to the *DDR* when his life turned yet another corner into despondency. His short-lived liaison with Ralph Werner had left him nearly broke and without a home. He obtained a permit to visit his ailing relatives in a small town in East Germany and for three and a half years he lived illegally in the *Deutsche Demokratische Republik*.

The old *Trabi* he had inherited from his uncle, just made it into town and then died. Ulli was not one of the visitors who came with money. Sixty years old, he had no choice but to apply for welfare assistance and take up residence in a home for the elderly, run by the *Heilsarmee*. The humiliation, the unhealthy living conditions and the lack of social contacts gave him no incentive to prolong his life. He died of loneliness and deprivation before the official reunification of the two Germanys in October of the following year. Manfred paid for the funeral services and the cremation of his remains.

After the first weeks of pandemonium, order gradually returned to Schlutup. The euphoria subsided and reality began to overshadow the new situation in West Germany. Thousands had come to stay, to breathe the air of freedom from oppression and to live the dream of economic and social well-being.

The Federal Republic of Germany shouldered an enormous burden. Unemployment in Schlutup neared twenty per cent and voters demanded new leadership. Manfred Scholte's last year in office was his toughest.

"How quickly people turn away from you when things don't go their way," he commented to Karl Berger one evening. "All the years of good fortune are forgotten."

Karl, who had finally retired earlier that year, said, "You have been a good mayor and they will remember that in the future."

"Yeah, a monument would be nice." He laughed half-heartedly. "Me on a pedestal!"

The local elections coincided with the one-year anniversary of the reunification in October of 1991. Manfred Scholte's name was not on the ballot. As he had promised his wife, he did not run for reelection.

"It is timely for me to quit," he declared in an interview with the press. "I have done for this town all I could for over a quarter century." He relapsed into his former stilted way of speaking. "A new era is upon us, and a new era requires a new leadership. Whatever the outcome of the election, I will support the new mayor."

Frieda suggested it was time for a celebration. "There is a lot to celebrate, once you are a private citizen. We will have a party like never before; let's invite the whole town."

Her husband was less enthusiastic. "Let's keep it within the boundaries of reality." He still spoke as if to the reporter. "Don't forget, Fritz Wendt is the man of the hour. There are those who might no longer feel inclined to rub elbows with me."

Fritz Wendt, who had run almost unopposed, became the new mayor of Schlutup. His victory reception at the *Hotel Zum Anker* was topped the following weekend by Manfred Scholte's farewell party, held in the large banquet room of the *Neue Konvention Halle*.

The festivities honoring the outgoing mayor, celebrating his nearly three decades in City Hall, were in full swing. There were speeches by Deputy Mayor Borge, the chief of police, and political as well as personal friends. Mayor-elect Fritz Wendt congratulated Manfred Scholte for his successful years in office and thanked the people of Schlutup for the confidence they bestowed in him. He waved to the crowd as he left the podium.

Kurt Lansen stepped up to the dais and began his address under enthusiastic applause. "Meine Damen und Herren…" A shot rang out and the revered teacher sank to the floor of the podium.

A second of absolute silence. Then a burst of confused outcries and tumultuous rushing to the raised platform. Others ran to the door. Police present for the celebration tried to gain control. Paramedics pushed through the crowd to the steps leading to the podium, upsetting tables and chairs. Manfred and Karl helped Ilse up the few steps to reach her husband who lay on the floor. Supporting himself on one elbow, Kurt looked in bewilderment toward the wide-open double doors on the side of the hall. A dark stain formed beneath the left lapel of his suit jacket. "Why, Wolfgang…" he said.

Ambulance personnel carrying a stretcher worked their way through the confused multitude and up the steps. Kurt still stared at the man in a rumpled suit standing in the door.

Wolfgang Johannsen surrendered the revolver without a struggle and held out his hands to the officer who handcuffed him. Ambulance personnel rushed Kurt on the stretcher out of the hall. As they passed through the door, Wolfgang lowered his head and murmured, " I am sorry, Kurt."

Within minutes the ambulance arrived at the emergency entrance to the municipal hospital. At the *Neue Konvention Halle* and in the plaza in front of it citizens, in shock and in disbelief over what had just happened, were slow to comprehend. Police cleared the way as officers led the perpetrator to a police car. "Clear the building and go home!" a voice came through a loudspeaker. Confused, not yet wanting to believe what they had witnessed, the people of Schlutup followed the orders and dispersed.

***

Kurt Lansen, beside his teaching job, had served on the school board during mayor Scholte's last term in office. Against the consensus that Wolfgang Johannsen should be replaced as custodian, Kurt had always found a way to keep him on. Wolfgang lost his protector when Kurt retired, and he was fired.

Misdirected resentment, building over months, led Wolfgang to commit the odious act against his sole benefactor. The years of living in an unforgiving, corrupt society and shunned on his return to Schlutup by most of his former peers, had their effect on his judgment. A desperate man, isolated and in conflict within himself, he lashed out irrationally and struck who might have been his only friend.

Initial interrogation revealed little as to his motive, although Wolfgang gave his full cooperation. Calm and polite, he answered questions as best he could: the revolver had been his father's in the first World War; his pension was sufficient to cover his needs; the assistance program helped with the rent for his one-room apartment. "I have no ill feelings toward anybody," he said several times, calmly and respectfully.

While awaiting trial, Wolfgang was ordered to undergo psychiatric evaluation. From his prison cell he sent a letter of apology to Ilse Lansen. "I am very sorry to have inflicted such pain and sorrow on Kurt and on you, who have been kind to me when no one else was. I will forever regret my crime. May Kurt recover from the wound I caused him."

Kurt recovered slowly from the gunshot wound Wolfgang had inflicted on him. The bullet had lodged itself millimeters from the heart, missing the aorta by a hair.

"A more powerful weapon might have propelled the bullet through the body to exit at the back, but it could have done more damage to the lung and possibly hit the spine," the chief surgeon at the municipal hospital explained to Ilse. "So, we don't know... it could have been better, but it also could have been much worse."

Two extremely delicate operations had been necessary: one to remove the bullet, the second to stop an internal bleeding that had resulted from the first operation. The hospital could not release him to go home for several months, into the new year.

When the sun warmed the air for a few days in March, Ilse accompanied him on his first walks outdoors. He was not in pain, but breathing was difficult for him and the leg muscles had been inactive for almost half a year so that he had to relearn how to walk.

"Ilse, it is useless—useless to be angry at Wolfgang. The burden he carries around with him is heavy—heavier than mine." Kurt's breath came in short gasps.

"You are a generous and forgiving man, and I love you for it."

"His youthful error to—to embrace Communism, only to come to the realization of his—his mistake thirty years later… Can you imagine how hard it must be to live—to live with that?" A strand of hair that had turned white fell over his forehead.

"It has destroyed him." Softly Ilse pushed his hair back.

"Yes. And that's why he isolated himself. Couldn't believe that—that anyone would accept him. He didn't see that we, most of us, were willing to forgive and forget. In the end, it drove him to act… act out in desperation."

"What will happen to him? And, dear, don't talk too much; it makes you tired."

Kurt ignored her caution. "He will have to agree to a plea of insanity. He might have to spend the rest of his life in a mental institution."

Ilse wanted to end the conversation so Kurt could catch his breath. "The trial is to begin next month," she said.

"The case is not complicated. He confessed; there are a hundred witnesses, there is no conspiracy. He acted on his own." Kurt continued, although he needed all his strength to do so. "They will try to keep him locked up, but—I'll do what I can to prevent that. Perhaps… perhaps psychiatric supervision, something like that. Putting him in jail… What good would that do? I have no feelings of revenge."

"How old is he? You know?"

"He's sixty-seven, I believe. He's not going to do harm to any-one."

In the months that followed the deplorable incident at the convention hall, and after handing over the reigns of the city to Fritz Wendt, Manfred and Frieda went on an extended vacation in the Austrian Alps, northern Italy and Switzerland.

Manfred Junior lacked the social skills of his father. He did not care for a career in politics; he possessed, however, a keen sense of business and intended to take over the leading role in his father's firm. When his parents returned from their holiday tour, they learned that he had fired the general manager of the hardware store chain.

"What happened? I trusted Richard Groth, he was with the firm almost from the beginning."

"He is an asshole, wanted to tell me how to run the business. When he closed a deal on wire cables with *Rhurtech Stainless,* without consulting me, I had to let him go. He just couldn't accept the idea that I was his boss."

"Manfred, the man is sixty-five years old; he has experience. You are new; you have much to learn."

"He's also old-fashioned, Dad. Doesn't go with the time. We're sitting on a ton of half-inch wire cable, which *Ostsee Industrie* won't buy. The shipyard switched to the new titanium and carbon fibers."

Manfred had expected that there might be difficulties between his son and Richard Groth; they didn't teach social skills at university. With a master's degree in business, Manfred Junior thought he knew it all, but he did not have the experience of a lifetime in the hardware business. He was right about the steel cable; still, the older man's knowledge was priceless.

"With the federal retirement benefits and the pension plan you set up, he will be well provided for." Manfred Junior dismissed his father's concerns. "You are too soft on people. This is a business we are running here, not a charity."

"That's not the point," and under his breath, "Boy, you have to learn a lot about people."

The cobblestone plaza near the renovated freight station had been renamed *Manfred Scholte Platz*. In a small ceremony, Fritz Wendt made a speech and helped Manfred cut the ribbon. In attendance were former and present community leaders and guests. Ilse Lansen supported Kurt who insisted on congratulating his old friend personally.

Richard Groth came forward to shake Manfred's hand; he ignored Manfred Junior who stood beside his father.

Manfred held on to his hand. "Richard, will you and your wife join me and my family in a small reception this evening at my house, please?"

No reception had been planned for that evening at Manfred Scholte's residence; it was an impromptu gesture.

"Very kind of you, but we have another engagement," and he walked away.

Manfred turned to his son. "See what you have done?"

Wolfgang Johannsen's trial began the day after renaming the old plaza to be known henceforth as Manfred Scholte Platz. Sam Morgenstern, the defense attorney, addressed judge Moltke, presiding over the district court."Your Honor, Herr Johannsen acknowledges his guilt. He is remorseful and willing to submit himself to psychiatric care. We plead to have him released into the care of his psychiatrist."

The medical expert testified that, in his opinion, the defendant posed no threat to the community. "With proper supervision and continued counseling, he will be able to function normally. Incarceration would be counterproductive in this case." Wolfgang's court appointed psychiatrist continued, "his behavior as custodian at the trade school revealed him as an introvert, a harmless individual who one day snapped. His irrational action was the result of guilt he no longer was able to bear, but such impulses can easily be contained with medication and proper guidance." Then he brought up the long years Johannsen spent in the Soviet Union and the influence they may have had on his psyche.

Judge Moltke dismissed the last remarks of the psychiatrist's evaluation. "That has no bearing on the case. We will deal with the facts, not with presumptions that may or may not have led the accused to shoot Herr Lansen," he said gruffly.

On the third day of the trial, the judge declared, "I have heard enough and I am ready to rule in this case. But before I do so, Herr Lansen, would you like to say something?"

A court attendant assisted Kurt to the witness stand. "Yes, your Honor. I would like to make a statement." Seated, Kurt Lansen spoke, taking shallow breaths between short sentences. "Your Honor, I have known Herr Johannsen since... eh, for many, many years. He came to me for help after his return from—from the Soviet Union. I was able to help until—until I retired." After a short break, he continued. "Your Honor, I forgave him for his—for his deed. Perhaps the court... Perhaps the court can do the same."

"Thank you, Herr Lansen. The court will consider your conciliatory position. I will announce my decision on Monday morning."

The judge ordered Wolfgang Johannsen to be sent to the *Nervenanstalt*, the Mental Institution for the criminal insane, in Reindorf near Hamburg. After one year the court was to hear the evaluation report for further decisions.

***

Traffic on Highway 11 from München to Freising was moving at a fast pace. Hans-Peter and Ninotchka were driving north. A Skoda passed them. Another car switched into the passing lane in front of the Skoda to avoid a sudden slow-down. Running out of room, the driver of the Skoda was forced to hit the brakes. His car was struck from the rear and propelled into the car in front. More cars smashed into them and the Skoda ended up in a mangled, almost unrecognizable wreck. Tires screeched, horns blasted as more cars crashed, creating a pile-up of a dozen or more vehicles.

In a quick decision, Hans-Peter swerved onto the right shoulder and stopped. "Stay in the car," he cautioned Nina. Well to the side of the road, he got out of his Fiat convertible and ran to the badly beaten and twisted heap of cars. He made his way through the wreckage to the Skoda. Smoke came from under the hood. Hans-Peter saw immediately that the driver and the woman beside him were dead. In the back, in a safety seat, was a baby, apparently unhurt. His spontaneous reaction was to get to the crying infant. Doors jammed, he reached through the broken window and managed to undo the safety belt of the car seat. With the child in his arms, Hans-Peter ran between the stopped cars back to his Fiat, as the Skoda exploded.

"Take care of it, see that it is all right." He handed Ninotchka the baby and scrambled back to see where he could render assistance. As police, fire engines and ambulances arrived at the scene, he returned to his car.

Hans-Peter thought it best to drive with the baby directly to the hospital in Garching, back twelve kilometers. He got behind the wheel, turned around and followed an ambulance.

"Seems to be all right," Ninotchka said. "Why hospital?"

"Can't just take the baby. What are you thinking?"

He dropped Ninotschka and the baby off at the emergency entrance as more ambulances arrived and he returned to the crash site; with his military training, he believed he could make himself useful. Tow trucks and more ambulances had arrived, police directed traffic around the scene and in less than two hours, traffic on the two-lane highway was again running smoothly. Along the side and on the median strip, police were still taking information from drivers. Paramedics assisted people with minor injuries into an ambulance, and there was nothing more Hans-Peter could do. He returned to Garching and joined Nina in the waiting room of the hospital. Presently, a nurse brought the baby out of the examination room and told them, "She is all right, not even a bruise. It's like a miracle."

Nina reached out to take the child, but the nurse stepped back. "After confirming the death of her parents, we will have to list her as an orphan. She will stay at our facility until the authorities decide on her future welfare."

"But she be safe our home. My husband safe her life, pick out from burning car." Nina took a step toward the nurse, but Hans-Peter held her back.

A doctor came from the operating room where he attended crash victims. Nina stepped in his way. "Doctor, we safeted baby. We take care..."

"Ma'am, we have to follow procedures."

"I adopt her on the spot. I adopt right now. You hear? I adopt. Hanse-Pet, tell him."

"Nina, what are you saying? We have to think about that. The doctor is right."

"I adopt right here and now. I take care. Where is paper to sign?"

Of course, they left the hospital without the child, but Ninotchka had already made up her mind. "We will have the baby, Hanse-Pet. She is sweet. Eighteen months, doctor guess. I already have name for her: is Nina, after me. Nina, you know, like me? No Ninotchka—is too long. Nina Hauser. She has dark hair, like me— only now is blonde, you know."

"That may take a long time." Hans-Peter fondled the beard he had begun to grow. "I kind of like the idea. Us, a baby? Can you imagine?"

"I can imagine. Why you ask?"

Every day Ninotchka made the ten-kilometer trip to the hospital. In a few weeks her petition to adopt baby Nina came back from the adoption agency. At first reading it was a crushing blow. The *Jugendamt*, handling adoption applications, objected to Hans-Peter as suitable father because of his age. **"While there is no age limit, we prefer adoptive parents under fifty years."** Then there was another clause. **"Research into the identity of the deceased parents and the child revealed that the Trzebiez family is of Polish nationality, residing in the city of Katowice."**

Nina's face lit up. "We move Poland. I tell you, we move Poland. And I'm no old, only forty-six. You old man, sixty-six. Read more."

Hans-Peter picked up the letter. **"No known relatives. Frans Trzebiez: parents and siblings killed in Warsaw uprising, Mirna Trzebiez: no apparent relations."**

"We go *Jugendamt*. Get up. Let's go. We go right away." Nina pulled Hans-Peter on the sleeve. "We tell them, I Polish. Come on, or you too old? Don't let them see you old man. You no old."

A couple of days after their urgent visit to the agency, Hans-Peter and Ninotchka received the paper that entitled them to take the infant home as **"temporary foster parents"**. Ninotchka had been busy buying everything a baby needs and converting their second bedroom into a baby room, with crib, dresser and bassinette.

Nina Hauser had never let on that she wanted to be a mother and Hans-Peter did not know of her hidden longing. This sudden revelation came as a surprise to both of them and their world changed the moment baby Nina entered their home.

"Temporary, huh? They don't know Ninotchka Hauser. Temporary... I will be real mamuchka."

Six months later Hans-Peter and Ninotchka Hauser announced to their friends that they were the proud parents of a two-year old girl, named Nina.

Hans-Peter resigned from his post as general manager of *Wach und Schliessgesellschaft* and, according to Ninotchka's wishes, they prepared to move to Katowice in Poland.

They exchanged the aging Fiat for a Volkswagen *Vanagon* and gave up their residence in Munich. Unable to resist the temptation to show off their precious addition to the family, they drove north to Schlutup, stopping in Hannover at the Lietkes. Seeing his old antagonist so changed as a caring family man, Klaus had little difficulty putting rivalry aside and embrace him as a friend. Little Nina was delightful, speaking a mixture of Polish and German. Klaus and Helga had never met Ninotchka who contributed much to a fun-filled evening that brought even Klaus out of his usual somber mood.

The following day the Hausers arrived in Schlutup where Manfred and Frieda welcomed them in their home. Hans-Peter, whom nature had favored with the rare gift of youthfulness, couldn't hide his surprise to see Manfred as an old man.

"What happened to you, man? Half gray, half bald and dragging your feet?" He turned to Frieda. "How can you live with that man? Is he still able to get it up? I mean, look at him!"

They knew Hans-Peter and laughed. "As a father, one would think you have changed, but you're still the same old devil," said Frieda. "If he can't, I get it up for him!"

Ninotchka blurted out, "Hanse-Pet is same thing. I always get up for him!" Then she said more seriously, "but he is good father. You should see him. Good father."

Karl came in the evening with Krista.

"Here's another old man," Hans-Peter greeted him. "But that's okay, at least you stand straight up, not like our old pal Manfred." He gave Krista a tight hug.

"He may be old, but he is rich, so let him stoop a little," said Karl. "You look the same as in—when was it? 1980? Twelve years ago? Well, maybe not the same. What did you do with your hair? Put some color back in it, huh?"

"All natural. She's the one with the bleach bottle," giving Ninotchka a little shove.

"Seriously now, how is Kurt? It's almost been a year, hasn't it?"

"He's coming along," Manfred answered. "Trouble breathing. Ilse is marvelous, the way she stands by him." Then he asked, "You saw Klaus… How's he doing?"

"Still going to work every day—well, he is younger than all of us. Plans to retire next year. We finally hit it off, smoothed things over. He and Helga… They're both good people."

"You know about Ulli Bolt, no?" Frieda interjected. "Two years ago…."

"Yeah, I know. Poor guy. I always felt a little sorry for him."

The following day, Hans-Peter and Ninotchka visited Kurt and Ilse. "Silver gray! Looks good on you," Hans-Peter greeted him and gave Ilse a hug. "How are you?"

"I am all right. Wolfgang Johannsen is worse off than me," Kurt said. "Has one breakdown after another. His nerves are shot. An emotional wreck."

"Where is he?"

"In Reindorf, in the *Nervenanstalt* for the criminally insane. He's supposed to come out next year. I doubt it."

While Hans-Peter remained as guest in the Scholte household, Ninotchka traveled ahead with her daughter to find a place to live in Katowice.

The population of the city, formerly called Kattowitz, is half German and half Polish. It is the largest city in Silesia and thriving on the coal and steel industry.

Efficient and resolute, Ninotchka located a house for rent with the option to buy, on the outskirts of Katowice. Enthusiastically she told Hans-Peter on the telephone, "Come and see, you will love it. Is big with three bedroom, garden and Carpathian Mountain. Is ideal."

"What—it has mountains?"

"Not in the house. You dumb or something? You see mountain, not far. You see Carpathian Mountain."

"I love it already. And I love you. How is Nina?"

"She speak Polish already, like me. Polish. But also Deutsch, like me." Over his laughter she said, "Come soon," and then hung up.

***

Fritz Wendt and Manfred Scholte had no animosity between them, but some in the new hierarchy of city administration felt envious of the rich and still revered former mayor, looking for opportunities to discredit him.

On the day Hans-Peter said good-bye to his friends in Schlutup and left for Katowice to join Ninotchka and their daughter, the police moved in on Manfred Scholte Junior, whose private activities had been under surveillance for some time. On the tip from a neglected girlfriend he was arrested for possession of cocaine and other drugs.

The press reported the story on the front page and it immediately became the prime topic. In his penthouse apartment on the west side of town, the thirty-one year old bachelor had entertained the young elite of Schlutup to parties and orgies that came to the attention of the neighbors in the luxury high-rise, and ultimately of the authorities.

The most disturbing surprise for Frieda and Manfred was to discover that their daughter, Birgit, had attended some of her brother's parties. Without making her presence in Schlutup known to her parents, she flew in from Paris on several occasions to take part in gay and lesbian orgies at her brother's residence.

Manfred, using his influence as the former mayor, effected the release of his son, vouching for him to appear before the judge on the trial date specified by the court. He retained the best attorney, Sam Morgenstern, to defend his son.

"Herr Scholte, homosexuality was illegal in Germany since 1871 under paragraph 175 of the German Criminal Code, but that law was repealed in 1968," Sam Morgenstern explained. "Since then, Germany became one of the most tolerant countries and homosexuality is widely accepted. You don't have to concern yourself with that."

"That's a relief," Manfred exhaled; to him the shame of both his children being *schwul* was a far greater disgrace than the use of illegal drugs.

"Now, the cocaine thing is a different matter," Sam Morgenstern continued. "We have to plead that guests at his parties brought the stuff in without his knowledge. He then has to reveal a list of those people. They will have to get their own lawyers."

"When can you talk with him, Herr Morgenstern?"

"You can send him right over. I'll make room for him this afternoon."

"What about my business? Will it suffer?"

"I recommend you remove your son from the general manager's position. Make that clear in an interview with the *Schlutup News*."

The headline in the morning paper read, **"Richard Groth reinstated as General Manager of Scholte Concern"**.

"What were you thinking?" Manfred Scholte was outraged. "You ruined your life and took my company down with you. Our good name is on the line."

"If you look back, our good name isn't all that good. You think people have forgotten that incident with Gerd Schenker you were involved in?"

"Don't you dare bring that up. Besides, it's not true. I had nothing to do with what he did later, and you know it."

"Anyway, you didn't have to fire me. And for your information: I am not gay. I'm as straight as they come. Don't confuse me with Birgit."

Calmer, Manfred asked, "What's all that talk about then? The orgies?"

"You are a little behind the times, Dad. There were just some gays and bisexuals. No big deal. They might have been a little careless on the balcony or in the hallway at one time."

"You'll have to disclose some names. To clear yourself of the cocaine charges."

"I can't do that. It would backfire throughout the town. There are people involved, you won't believe."

"Under no circumstances will I let you go to jail. You have to cooperate with Sam Morgenstern. Judge Moltke will do his best to send you to prison."

"Morgenstern is good. He already told me, I'd probably get off with a hefty fine…"

"…Which I will have to pay. How much is he talking about?"

"No idea. Hefty, he said. I'll pay for it, if you let me keep my job."

"No. It's too late for that. You go back to university and become a lawyer."

***

Six months and two hundred fifty thousand marks later, the case was forgotten. Manfred Junior, on his father's demand, applied for law school. Birgit never again sat foot in her parent's house.

"I saved the boy, but we lost our daughter." Manfred had a soft spot for her.

"She's better off in Paris," was Frieda's reply. "There is no place for her in this town. These small-minded people will never understand. What do you say, we take a trip to Paris? I think that would be good, don't you think so?"

"I can't leave Richard alone. He just started again. There's a lot of catching up to do."

"I don't mean right now. Maybe in the summer? Paris would be nice in the summer."

"And what makes you think she will want to see us?"

"Oh, if we just see her once, tell her that we still love her. We won't interfere with her... You know. Her life is in a different world. Fashion—what do we know from fashion? It's a different world."

"Maybe next month."

The law school of the Humboldt University in Berlin accepted Manfred Junior and he was to start his first semester in the spring of 1993. There had been no more incidents of wild partying. At least, there had been no complaints. His father allowed him a small amount of pocket money and made the mortgage payments on the apartment.

"He'll cost me a truckload of money. At least six years until he can start earning."

"By then he'll be thirty-seven years old." Frieda thought about that. "That's not too old to begin a career as a lawyer, huh?"

"Too old? What's too old? Better late than never. He'll be a good lawyer."

In the summer, after Manfred Junior moved to Berlin, his parents made good on their plan for a vacation in Paris. Frieda notified Birgit that they were coming.

"Don't be alarmed, dear," her mother told her on the phone. "We are not barging in on you. We booked a suite in the Pavillon de la Reine. It's near the Centre George Pompidou —I don't know how to pronounce it. I am sure you know where that is." Frieda felt a little insecure talking to her worldly, sophisticated daughter. "It would be nice if you could spare an afternoon... If you have the time. And if not..."

Birgit interrupted her. "Sure, I'm glad you're coming. I am busy, but spring collection is out, so I can make myself free for a couple of hours. We already start on the fall and winter *couture*— it's a constant rat race."

The phone call left Frieda uncertain. "I don't know what to say. She's so... so above us," she told her husband. "How can we even talk to her?"

"We can talk to her all right. We're her parents, for Christ's sake. She better not talk that fancy French with us." His rough tone did not match the inner feelings he had for his daughter. "She better remember her humble beginnings right here in this provincial little town." His anger was unconvincing and Frieda knew it.

"Yes, yes, I know. But don't be so hard on her."

"No." A tear formed in the corner of his eye. "You know I won't be."

Manfred Scholte's hardware business was again in the capable hands of Richard Groth. He was able to negotiate an export contract with a shipyard in Spain and wangle a reasonable profit from the wire cable deal that had cost him his job the year before.

In the ten days they spent in Paris, Manfred and Frieda saw their daughter twice. Birgit had met them in the lounge of their hotel the day they arrived, and a second time on their last day in a café on the Champs Elysee near her office.

The days in between, they explored the city by themselves. One day they took a river cruise on the Seine, another they went to Montmartre and visited the Sacre Coeur. Frieda had ordered tickets in advance for a show at Moulin Rouge, which they both hated. The best day was strolling through the Champ de Mars. Manfred had insisted on going up the Eiffel Tower, but Frieda had no stomach for great heights, so she stayed behind enjoying an afternoon in the Jardin du Luxembourg.

At noon on the day before they left, in the café near her office, Birgit told them, "I have only half an hour."

Their meetings with Birgit had been awkward. She interrupted her talk often with epithets, such as "you won't understand" or "I can't explain" and used words common in the fashion industry but unfamiliar to her parents. She disclosed little of her life in the world of fashion, did not invite them to her apartment, nor tell them where it was.

Both her parents were intimidated by her alluring, worldly nonchalance and did not ask many questions. Each time after seeing her, they felt empty, rejected.

"Let's get out of here. I can't stand this town, this country, these French," Manfred complained. "They talk with their noses in the air and look down on you. Birgit is the same. 'Haut couture, manikins, glamour'—what the hell is she talking about? And those French names: 'Yves this or that, Dior, Chanel'—I tell you, we lost her. And no man in her life. All lesbians and gays, if you asked me. Can't wait to be on that plane tomorrow."

***

Returning from their vacation trip, Manfred found his business intact and thriving. After a short conference at his office with his re-appointed general manager, he returned home and dedicated himself to his hobby, the model railroad, spread out over the entire attic of his mansion. He needed time to put their Paris trip behind him.

"I wish we hadn't gone there," he told Frieda in the evening as they were going to bed. "Then I could still believe I had a daughter. Now…"

"Don't take it so hard. She's still our daughter."

"Damn it, she is; but she's not." He couldn't hide his anger and frustration. "This is not a normal family."

"My only regret is that we might never have grandchildren."

"Kurt and Ilse have no children and…" He hesitated. "Maybe we'd have been better off without them, too."

"Now, don't you talk like that."

"Okay, but you know who has a normal family? Klaus. That's a normal family. He and Helga have children and grandchildren. And now even Hans-Peter…"

"Isn't she the cutest little thing, that Nina? Only Hans-Peter is more like a grandfather to that child."

"I know. He'll be seventy before she goes to Kindergarten."

"You see, that's not normal either. Let's try and find happiness with what we have. Don't be bitter. Birgit is still our daughter and

Manfred is going to be a fine lawyer some day. You'll see."
"Sure. I'm tired now. Tomorrow is another day. Good night."
"Good night, dear."

In the attic a Styrofoam mountain, housing a newly installed transformer, began to smolder. Green acrylic paint oozed down the slope onto the painted canvas that covered the wooden floor. A small orange flame licked the melting landscape beside the railroad track while Manfred and Frieda fell asleep in the bedroom directly below.

***

Nearing the end of the twelve-month term of Wolfgang Johannsen's confinement, the chief psychiatrist from the *Nervenanstalt* presented his evaluation to the court. His report concluded that "the patient poses no threat to others or to himself" and that there was no reason to keep him at the facility. Consequently, Johannsen was released under the condition of continued psychiatric counseling and periodic reports to be filed with the court.

Wolfgang Johannsen moved into the same home for the elderly that had provided room and board for Ulrich Bolt until his death in 1990. Under the auspices of the *Heilsarmee*, the sixty-nine year old had little to live for and did not wait for death to come to him. He managed to hang himself with a bed sheet on a bracket for the heating pipe that ran under the ceiling of his room.

The incident was hardly newsworthy and appeared in the paper as one paragraph under the heading, **W. Johannsen dead at age sixty-nine.** The article read: **Recently released from the mental institution at Reindorf, Wolfgang Johannsen committed suicide by hanging. He will be remembered as the would-be assassin of Kurt Lansen in October of 1991. Herr Lansen survived the attempt.**

The same edition of the Schlutup News reported much more prominently on the fire that destroyed the entire upper floor of former mayor Manfred Scholte's mansion. **Herr and Frau Scholte**

Scholte were the only occupants in the house. Both survived unharmed. It is believed that the fire was caused by the faulty installation of a transformer.

Acrid smoke had roused the two sleepers shortly after midnight. Manfred was immediately aware that he had forgotten to turn off the main switch that controlled the circuits of his elaborate model train system. He hurried upstairs and, opening the door to the attic, was met by a raging inferno.

"We have to get out," he urged Frieda who gathered clothing from the wardrobe. "No time for that." He ran downstairs to his study to collect documents from his desk and file cabinet.

Frieda, fully dressed, met him in the hall. "Put your clothes on, dear. Don't let them find you half naked."

Fire trucks arrived in less than five minutes. Manfred and Frieda stood across the street. Among neighbors and onlookers they watched as firefighters climbed the ladder with the hose and began spraying water through a broken attic window. On one side the wooden beams were burning and part of the roof collapsed.

The fire was extinguished in a short time, thanks to neighbors who had seen smoke coming from the roof of the Scholtes' home and called the fire department. Manfred, accompanied by the fire chief, climbed the stairs to the top floor and they found the attic completely devastated. The railroad, Manfred's pride, was in shambles. "I must have forgotten to turn off the main switch," said Manfred.

"You were lucky neighbors called us so soon," said the chief, looking at the damage. "Our report will state that the fire was of electrical origin. A poorly insulated, overheating transformer ignited the foam rubber landscape. You'll get a copy for the insurance. You have insurance, right, Herr Scholte?"

"Yes, no problem there. It's just... the model railroad is thousands of marks. The love and labor that went into it cannot be replaced."

"Sorry about that, Herr Scholte."

The second story, where the bedrooms and guest rooms were, was rendered useless due to water damage, and even the ground floor had sustained some damage. Water was dripping through the ceiling and running down the walls, however, most of the furniture and belongings could be salvaged.

Acrid smell left by the fire permeated the house. "You won't be able to live here for some time," the chief told Frieda who stood in the middle of the dining room.

Work began immediately to replace the roof and restore the upper floor of their house. Manfred and Frieda moved into the penthouse on the top floor of one of Manfred's buildings, which he had not rented out but used as a tax write-off. They saw the benefit of living in an apartment. Their house was much too big for just the two of them and they considered selling it.

"I always thought of this apartment for Manfred when he would get married and have a family. This would be perfect for a little family. But I have my doubts that he will ever want to come back and live in Schlutup."

"We have already done enough for the kids," Manfred answered. "He will cost me another hundred thousand marks over the next five or six years."

"Birgit doesn't need our help anymore." Frieda had tears in her eyes. "She wouldn't even want it."

***

Gudrun's affair with Hans-Peter had ended soon after the Gang expelled him for having betrayed one of the members. Just twenty-one years old and left with a penchant for sensual pleasures, she found that there was nothing wrong with accepting gifts for sexual favors. Before long, she quit her inadequately paid job at the railroad freight station that interfered with the pursuit of her newfound hobby.

She rented a room above the nightclub *Rote Katze* in downtown Schlutup and word of her talents spread among the male population. Before the end of the first month at the *Rote Katze* she struck a deal with the proprietor of the club and took over the entire upper floor of the building. Properly registered as "*Bei Gudrun*", her business shifted into high gear, employing first two, then three and soon six equally talented young women. Her own special favors she reserved for special customers.

Madam Gudrun, who continued to use only her first name, became a rich woman and moved to a better neighborhood. In her mid-forties, she changed her business to a high-class call girl ring under the name "Gudrun's Personal Services". The English designation gave her enterprise a certain exclusiveness, intended for a sophisticated, up-scale clientele. Her expensive business cards bore the logo of an embossed red cat, reminiscent of her beginnings at the *Rote Katze*.

In the fall of 1993, when Gudrun was sixty-six years old, she bought the renovated and beautifully refurbished mansion Manfred and Frieda Scholte had put up for sale.

Located in the residential Westside of Schlutup, she converted the ground floor of the stately villa into a respectable "Gentlemen's Club" and arranged the upper story as her apartment with dining room, living room, salon for entertaining, kitchen with pantry and her private bedroom suite. The top floor she had rebuilt into six bedrooms, each with bath, for her associates: attractive, classy young women of exquisitely fine manners, each of them educated and fluent in at least two languages. As she had put on excess weight and increased her girth considerably, Gudrun equipped her mansion with an interior elevator.

Such exclusive clubs, frequently encountered in residential neighborhoods of German cities, are generally not looked upon as distasteful. Discrete and run in an orderly fashion, they coexist with less refined bordellos and street prostitutes in the poorer sections of town, all of which are legalized and government controlled.

Gudrun was a respected entrepreneur. She paid her taxes, made sizable contributions to charities and treated her associates as equals. She owned a fleet of limosines for the use by her associates to meet their gentlemen callers, or to pick up customers, whom she preferred to call her guests. Often cars with Hamburg or Berlin license plates, their chauffeurs napping in the driver's seats, parked in spaces marked "reserved".

Mayor Fritz Wendt, a confirmed bachelor, was a regular at Madam Gudrun's. Born in 1948 at the time of Germany's economic revival, Fritz studied first medicine, then psychology and finally political sciences. His wealthy parents supported his zest for learning, but he showed no inclination to put any of his acquired knowledge to good use until 1991 when he decided to run for mayor of Schlutup. With Manfred Scholte out of the race, he had won easily and discovered he had an ability to lead, combined with a charismatic personality.

In the quaint, yet elegant atmosphere of The Club, he often held informal meetings with business tycoons, financial advisors and political strategists. As a result, Schlutup blossomed into an industrial city and its population grew over the next decade to more than 75,000.

Klaus Lietke had sent Manfred a note, after he learned of the fire that caused so much damage to his home. A few months later he read an article in the *Spiegel* about the sale of the house, and he was outraged.

"Helga, read this," he turned to his wife. "I can't believe it." He folded the magazine and handed it to her.

There was a picture of the mansion. Helga read: **Schlutup, October 20, 1993. Mayor's villa sold to "Gudrun's Personal Services". After a fire had nearly destroyed it, the well-known Madam Gudrun bought the restored mansion of former mayor Manfred Scholte for an undisclosed amount. The stately building is now the home of the prestigious "Gentlemen's Club".**

"Gudrun? *The* Gudrun? Are you sure?" Helga was perplexed.

"Sure. I have known for a long time that she became a prostitute. She began turning tricks soon after Hans-Peter left her. Schwarzer told me."

"So you knew she was like... like that?"

"No, not until she got involved with Hans-Peter. He could corrupt anyone. I'm not saying it was his fault. She must have had it in her."

Helga, who had never seen Gudrun, formed a certain image of her. "You must have known, Klaus, that she was... promiscuous.

Men know that. Did you ever...?"

"No!" He protested. "I was eighteen, nineteen. The war... We had other worries. I've never had a girlfriend. I didn't know anything about girls."

"What did she look like? Long hair? Walked around in short skirts? Makeup? What?"

"Are you jealous of something that happened nearly fifty years ago? You know me better than that. And nothing ever happened. Never! Until I met you. And we waited until we were married."

"I know. I'm just teasing you. Don't get upset."

"I'm not upset. It's just... I can't believe Manfred sold to *her*. He knew about her... and me. And Hans-Peter."

"She must have offered a higher price. *Those* women are rich."

"Still..."

The thought of her husband and Gudrun titillated her slightly. That evening they made love—a rare occasion for the couple, now in their later years and rather uninspired in the game of sex.

Kurt Lansen read the story in the Schlutup News. "Should I send the article to Klaus?" he asked Ilse. "I think he would like to know."

"I don't know," she said. "It may upset him. And what about Helga?"

"After all these years? But, yeah, maybe you're right. He'll find out anyway. It's in all the tabloids."

"We should tell Hans-Peter. He's not getting all the news from here in Poland."

"I'll send him the clipping. He's gonna get a kick out of this."

Karl Berger and Krista had coffee with Manfred and Frieda in their living room. It was a blustery late autumn day, so they did not make use of the terrace overlooking the quaint old center of Schlutup.

Karl, nearing his seventy-fourth birthday, had become frail and he depended heavily on Krista. "I think you made the right decision to give up that big house, but why did you have to sell to her?" he reproached Manfred.

"Look, Karl," Manfred explained. "She paid me a good fifty thousand more than the next highest bidder. I am no longer as rich as people think. Junior cost me a bundle; now I pay for his law school; I pay Richard a hefty sum and business has not been as good as in the seventies and eighties. Not to mention the mayor's income of hundred twenty thousand..."

"People talk, is all I am saying."

"Karl, most people will agree with me: she's an asset to the community. She pays taxes, is generous with contributions, employs a staff of half a dozen, not counting the girls, eh... ladies."

"But Manfred," Frieda interjected, "I noticed a few of the ladies of my church group avoided me lately. Karl is right; they're talking behind my back, I'm sure."

"Bunch of hypocrites, all of them. I told you many times: stay away from that church. Nothing but gossip. They are the worst."

"But you also said to be active in the community..."

"Not in the church. I told you that."

Krista nudged Karl. "Come on, Karl, let's go home. You're falling asleep," and to Frieda, "he's always tired lately, and so cold. His hands are always like ice cubes. Call us a cab; he won't make it walking."

In the cab, Karl dozed off and on arrival at their home, Krista could not wake him. He had quietly gone into a permanent sleep.

Krista directed the cab driver to the municipal hospital.

***

The remaining members of the Gang of Seven came together for the funeral of their leader from the early days in the garden shack.

Manfred and Frieda were there. Ilse assisted Kurt to a seat next to them in the front row of the little chapel. Hans-Peter came alone all the way from Katowice. Klaus Lietke and Helga drove up from Hannover.

The coffin was richly covered with wreaths and flowers from his many friends and dignitaries of the city government.

Fritz Wendt held the eulogy, pointing out the services Karl Berger had rendered to the town of Schlutup as a member of the city council. Others followed, and then Manfred spoke of the long friendship he had with the deceased.

There was no priest or pastor. Krista was Lutheran, but had not set foot in a church for as long as she had lived with Karl, nearly fifty years. He had no religious affiliation and she knew he would not have cared for a religious ceremony.

Some eyes filled with tears as the coffin rolled slowly, noiselessly through an opening double door into the crematory, hidden in the darkness beyond.

Manfred and Frieda had prepared a small reception at their apartment for the inner circle of close friends and associates. Mayor Wendt assured Krista, "Karl's pension will continue, albeit somewhat reduced. There is also a fund for widows of city employees my predecessor has initiated. Technically, you are not a widow, but under a new provision in the municipal regulations you will be eligible to receive a small monthly allowance."

Manfred who stood nearby added, "Don't worry, Krista, we'll take care of you."

"Thanks. I don't wanna have to go to the *Heilsarmee*. That's where people die or hang themselves. First Ulli Bolt and then just a couple of months ago that… that lunatic Johannsen. I don't wanna end up dead like them."

How typical of Krista, thought Frieda who had joined them. With a warm smile she said, "Anything we can do… We'll be there for you."

Ilse and Helga nodded their agreement and Klaus came up to them. "Karl always looked out for me since the early days. He and Kurt were my best friends. I will never forget that."

"Hey, I'm not dead yet!" Kurt, having trouble with his breathing, laughed weakly and smoothed his silver-gray hair away from his forehead . To Krista he said, "We'll all take care of you, as you took care of us back in the garden house."

Hans-Peter who was talking with mayor Wendt, looked over to Kurt, the only one sitting. "Don't exert yourself, we don't want you to be next," he said in his whimsical, mischievous way. He pulled a chair next to Kurt's and sat down. "Kurt, I've had this on my mind for a long time. I never held it against you that you threw me out. You did what you had to do. I just wanted to tell you that."

"I didn't throw you out, Hans-Peter. It was a group decision.

As you said: I did what I had to do."

"I always respected you."

"Thanks for saying that." It seemed Kurt's breath came more easily, as if Hans-Peter's acknowledgment had lifted a weight off his chest. "Thank you." More animatedly he added, "Why didn't you bring your wife?"

"Ah, she has Nina, you know. She's three and a handful. She's so full of life, has Ninotchka's spirit. We are so lucky to have her."

"As long as she's not taking after you," Kurt smiled.

Hans-Peter grinned. "Why? What's wrong with me?" Ilse tapped her husband on the shoulder. "Let's go, Kurt. It's been enough for you." To Hans-Peter she said, "Give our best to both your Ninas. Kurt needs to rest now."

Snow flurries swirled in the light breeze this early November evening as they stepped out into the street. Klaus had his car parked at the curb. With the snow, their drive back to Hannover would take longer than three hours.

The mayor's limousine pulled up and the chauffeur opened the door for Krista, Kurt and Ilse. At her house, Fritz Wendt walked Krista to the door and then dropped Kurt and Ilse off at the entrance to their apartment building.

Hans-Peter, as usual, was a guest at Manfred and Frieda's home. "How about a nightcap, huh?" Manfred asked. "Remember the cheap stuff we used to drink back in the forties? Man, how could we even stand it?"

"*Wacholder*. Nobody touches *Wacholder* anymore. Hey, we were young, what did we know?"

"Here, have some of this." Manfred produced a bottle and two glasses. "Twelve-year old Scotch. It won't kill you."

They sipped the smooth liquor. Hans-Peter grew pensive. "Karl is gone. You and Kurt are the only ones left in this town now. If Ninotchka didn't insist on going back to Poland, I might have wanted to settle in Schlutup."

"It's not the same anymore. Look how it's growing."

"Still... The old memories..." Thoughtfully, he swallowed some of his whisky. "This is good stuff," and after a pause, "Karl didn't like to drink, remember?"

"Oh, he drank a beer or two, but he never touched *Schnaps*." Manfred lowered his head. "What a good man he was. Seventy-four... that's too young to die. Cancer... and they never knew. Krista said he hated the doctors, never went for a check-up."

They clinked glasses.

Frieda joined them. "Krista will be all right, I think. How old is she?

"She's about my age. Karl brought her over in '46 when she was twenty, twenty-one. So she must be sixty-seven, sixty-eight now."

"Didn't change much, except for the gray hair," said Hans-Peter. He emptied his glass. "I want to get going early in the morning. It's an eight to ten hour trip, depending on the traffic at the border. They're so slow, those customs people."

"Yeah, let's call it a night."

***

A light dusting of snow covered the streets and parks of Schlutup on the day Karl would have celebrated his seventy-fourth birthday.

Manfred shook the flurries from his hat. "Let's not stay too long. This might turn into a blizzard," he said to Frieda as she rang the doorbell.

"Nice of you to come," Krista greeted them at her door. "Look at all them flowers."

Her living room looked like a flower shop. "I didn't want 'em to go to waste over at the, the... you know. So I brought 'em home."

"Manfred told me not to bring any. You would have every vase full, he said—and he was right. Make us some tea, Krista; we brought cake. Didn't want you to be alone today, his birthday."

Manfred pulled a small flask from his coat pocket. "Arrack. Goes good with the tea."

"Thanks." Krista went into the kitchen to put the water on. Through the open door she told them, "I went to the garden colony this morning. You know, there's a fence around it now. The gate was closed for the winter, so I couldn't get in. I wanted to see the house… Forty-eight years… That's when me an' Karl…"

"Is it that long?" Frieda interrupted her.

"He wanted to get married on our fiftieth anniversary. He said that twenty-five years ago, too. 'Yeah, yeah', I said. 'Promises, promises…' I didn't care, really."

"We considered you married anyway," Manfred threw in.

"He did go behind my back, in the early days. Remember Elsa? That got him in bad trouble. Almost landed him in Siberia. I never said nothin', but I didn't forget either. We was young…"

"Oh, I remember. He was lucky. They took his buddy Walter instead. Never heard from him again. Must have died in Siberia."

Frieda helped set the table. The conversation turned to more recent topics as they sat around the coffee table and Manfred said, "The town has grown so much and there is more crime. One of the first things Wendt did was to order that fence put up around the garden colony. Was a good thing, too. All that new industry he brings in drags a lot of riffraff with it."

"But Fritz Wendt is doing a good job," Frieda commented. "You said so yourself."

"Still, unemployment is high, and so is crime."

"That comes from progress. Karl always said, progress is two-sided. I didn't know what he meant, but now I do." Krista's thoughts returned to Karl, but Frieda wanted to take her mind elsewhere—that's what they had come for.

"Fritz Wendt is always at Gudrun's, they say. It's like he has an office there," she said. "All the important decisions he makes at her place, they say."

"What are you suggesting?" Manfred joked. "That I should have had an office there? That I would have been a better mayor?"

"He's a bachelor, Manfred. You? I would have gone straight to Sam Morgenstern and filed for divorce."

"So, then I should have…" Manfred chuckled and left that thought hanging in the air.

"Karl said he never went there, but I don't know," Krista mused.

"Naw, not Karl," Manfred shook his head. "Kurt… Now there I couldn't be sure."

"Now, let's not get into that. Ilse worries enough about him. Something's troubling him, she told me." Frieda tugged her husband lightly by the sleeve. "We'd better be going before the weather turns any worse," and to Krista, "Call us if you need anything."

"I'll be all right."

In the car on their way home, Manfred asked, "What about Kurt? What did Ilse say?"

"Nothing, only that he's often so absentminded."

"That all?"

***

Industry in Schlutup struggled to stay alive and unemployment remained high through the winter of 1993/94. The shipyard, an appliance company and the food distribution center cut personnel, but it was not worse than in most German cities.

Fritz Wendt did what he could and he had some success in attracting manufacturing firms that provided job opportunities. In the elegant, yet cozy atmosphere of Gudrun's Gentlemen's Club, he entertained the president of the *Hansawerke AG* that formerly had its headquarters in Schlutup. At last he was able to negotiate the return of a branch of that company to the city.

It was a small triumph, but the city of Schlutup applauded the mayor. Manfred Scholte congratulated Fritz Wendt by telephone. "Good job, Fritz. Our citizens are lucky to have you." Manfred searched his vocabulary for fancy words, as was his custom. "There is a glimmer of hope at the end of the tunnel," was all he came up with. "It's a promise for the future of Schlutup."

Wendt smiled into the receiver hearing his predecessor's excessive accolade. "Thank you, thank you. I know, you could have done it, too."

"I never set foot at Gudrun's—if that's what you mean. My wife would have divorced me! So, I couldn't have done it."

They both laughed. "Well, then thank Madam Gudrun for her civic mindedness."

Rebuilding of the old plant began in the spring and manufacturing of components for the Airbus started in early summer. When the design of the new A3XX came off the drawing board in June and the work force at the Hamburg plant soared to over 10,000, the local *Hansawerke* also took some additional workers and their families off the welfare list.

In this semi-prosperous summer of '94, when Schlutup experienced a mild comeback of a once healthy economy, a scandal rocked the town. Madam Gudrun was arrested for money laundering, drug trafficking and the illegal harboring and employment of undocumented aliens. A far-reaching investigation into her activities was likely to implicate persons heretofore known as solid citizens. The district court did not disclose names, but rumors had it that Mayor Fritz Wendt might be involved.

Sam Morgenstern, counsel to Madam Gudrun, effected her immediate release, based on her status of a businessperson who did not present a flight risk. The immigration authority, however, took three of her female employees in custody for deportation to their home countries, Yugoslavia, Latvia and the Ukraine. Madam Gudrun was placed under house arrest and had to report her whereabouts weekly.

In spite of the enormous impact on the community, the press received few details of this intriguing incident, which fueled speculation and gossip among the population of Schlutup and beyond.

Complicated machinations between the law firm of Morgenstern & Sons and the prosecution's attorneys resulted in dismissal of the money laundering charges. Clever bookkeeping showed clear details of her transactions and there were no discrepancies in her tax record. A second set of books that might have given a different picture remained hidden from the authorities.

With regard to the drug charges, Sam Morgenstern was unsuccessful in striking a deal with the prosecution. Typically, German courts make no distinction between soft and hard drugs and, while possession of small quantities for personal use does not constitute a crime, the acquisition does. Cases involving cannabis, or marijuana, are of low priority. For other illegal drugs, depending on amount and type, the law provides penalties of one month to four years imprisonment, in addition to a fine.

The violation of Immigration laws carries a monetary fine, a penalty Gudrun was prepared to pay.

Sam Morgenstern petitioned district Judge Moltke, presiding over the case, to excuse Madam Gudrun from appearing in court. "Your Honor, Madam Gudrun is in a state of poor health due to her obesity. Weighing in at two hundred kilos, she is rarely able to leave her home, except for visits to her doctor."

"Under the circumstances, presentation of sworn affidavits will suffice," Judge Moltke had to concede.

With that decision, Sam Morgenstern had won a victory even before the trial began. He had assured the judge's lenient disposition toward his client.

Fritz Wendt, known to have a close relationship with Madam Gudrun, had an informal conference behind closed doors with the judge. As was to be expected, no case could be established against him and the state's attorney was advised accordingly. Several clients —or guests, as the madam preferred to call them—were indicted for having either bought or sold cocaine, hashish and other controlled substances at Gudrun's establishment.

The local media tried to sensationalize the matter but had little information to keep the story going until weeks later when the case came to trial. Even then, those hoping for juicy tidbits were disappointed. The judge imposed a twenty-five thousand marks fine on an industrialist from the Rhineland, and two contractors working for *Hansawerke AG* received a thirty-day jail term and five thousand marks fine. All three had been found guilty of purchasing cocaine at the Gentlemen's Club.

On each of the three counts of immigration violations, Moltke imposed on Madam Gudrun a fine of twenty-five thousand marks—a mere slap on the wrist for her. On the drug violation, however, he did not let her get away so easily.

The presiding judge addressed Sam Morgenstern, Gudrun's legal representative. "In spite of recognizing her long, outstanding civic-minded generosity, I have no alternative but to find the defendant guilty of providing access to illegal controlled substances for sale at her premises. In lieu of a jail sentence, considering the poor state of health as attested by her personal physician, I sentence Madam Gudrun to a penalty of seven hundred thousand marks and the restrictions of her movements remain in effect until the fine is paid in full. Furthermore, I suspend her license to do business for one year." To the court attendant he motioned, "Remove the two defendants and take them to the holding cells for transfer to the city jail." The gavel hit the plate. "This court is adjourned."

Schlutup's inhabitants felt cheated out of juicy details they had expected from the process against Madam Gudrun, yet there were repercussions. The trial had lasted not more than two weeks, but the closure of the Gentlemen's Cub was discussed widely. What's the Madam doing now that The Club is shut down? What happened to the ladies? Would the two gentlemen return to work at the *Hansawerke* after their release from prison? Was Mayor Wendt actually involved? If so, how deeply?

Local and regional newspapers concentrated on that last question. Would Fritz Wendt last through the six-year term as mayor? Although no wrongdoing on his part was revealed, the rumors were a powerful agent. Support for him as Bürgermeister declined, and when in the following summer, after only a year in operation, the *Hansawerke* consolidated the manufacturing plant with the principal concern in Hamburg, his fate was sealed. Fritz Wendt chose to resign from office in August 1995 and Deputy Mayor Ferdinand Borge took over.

"His tenure as mayor lasted less than four years." Kurt leaned back in his chair. "Remember how enthusiastic people were? They couldn't wait for him to replace you. And you had the job for more than twenty-five years—longer, if you had wanted to."

They sat on the terrace of Manfred's penthouse apartment. "What will happen now?" Manfred was thinking aloud. "Another thirty people lost their jobs; some accepted transfer to Hamburg. What can Borge do?"

"Tough," replied Kurt. "He doesn't have Fritz' charisma. Hey, I heard Gudrun will reopen next month."

"Ferd's not exactly the type to go there."

"He should change his attitude and at least be friendly with her. It's important in this town. She plans an inauguration, a grand opening. You saw the ad in the paper, right?"

"Are you going?"

"I'm not invited. I'm not on her 'guest list'. Ilse wouldn't mind; she's pretty open about things like that. How about Frieda? She'd throw you out, huh?"

At that moment Frieda and Ilse came out to the terrace. "What are you talking about? Gudrun reopening? Look at you," Frieda mocked them, "old men, wanting to go to a whorehouse. It's ridiculous. They'd laugh their heads off!"

Ilse laughed so hard, she collapsed into a chair. "Go ahead, Kurt, maybe you learn some new tricks. You've been a little sluggish, you know."

Kurt grew silent as he often did lately, sometimes in mid-conversation, and Ilse regretted the remark she just made.

"We weren't talking about that," Manfred said seriously. "We talked about Ferdinand Borge. Maybe he should pay her a visit. Good politics."

"Borge? The old man will never be a replacement for Fritz Wendt." Frieda shook her head. "He just hasn't got it."

"Ferd Borge and Madam Gudrun? That's a joke!" Ilse stood up and turned to her husband. "Let's go, Kurt. You're brooding again. It's been long enough for you."

***

Manfred Scholte Junior returned to Schlutup in the fall of 1995 after completing four semesters of jurisprudence.

"Dad, this is not what I want to do. Corporate law—I have a good understanding of it. I could head the corporation, but I want to run for mayor. What do you say? Borge is old and decrepit, not the man to bring this town back to prosperity."

"Listen, son, what happened to you there in Berlin? You had no interest in politics, and now you want to be mayor? First of all, you're too young. I was thirty-eight when I became Bürgermeister, the youngest ever. Wendt was forty-three. You're only thirty-five."

Why don't you get your law degree first and then, if you still want it, go for it."

"Borge has two years to finish Wendt's term. In two years he can ruin the town. We need change. That's what I am thinking."

"Where do you get those revolutionary ideas? Is that what they teach you at Humboldt? Young man, that's not how we run this town, this country. I pay for your studies and you go back there and finish what you started. Then, in two years, if you still want to, go ahead. End of discussion."

Junior got up and mumbled, "old fashioned, behind the times, this town needs new blood, fresh ideas." He turned to his father, "Yes sir, as you wish. I'm on my way to becoming an old fart lawyer."

Against all expectations, Schlutup did not atrophy into a lifeless, decaying town. The shipyard and small manufacturing companies held their ground, though struggling. The fishing fleet added a third vessel and the packing plant employed seventeen workers.

Mayor Borge surprised everyone by offering a one-year tax-exempt incentive for new businesses relocating to Schlutup. As a result, an electrical appliance firm moved into the building the *Hansawerke* had vacated. Starting with a staff of only seven employees, the space was much too big, but the energetic management was growth-oriented.

"The old man is okay. Who would have thought…" the town's people commented.

"Yeah, but where will he get the revenue to run the city?" others doubted.

"I hear, he'll raise taxes on water, gas and electricity to make up for it."

"Smart man, but he will make enemies, too."

Such was the talk in the pubs, the public squares and in the families. The Schlutup News praised the Bürgermeister on the front page, and criticized him in the editorial column. The local trade school conducted a poll, questioning a thousand inhabitants of all walks of life and the result was astounding: the overwhelming majority of Schlutup's population gave the mayor high marks of approval.

Richard Groth announced his resolve to retire, come January 1996. He had joined Manfred's hardware business forty years ago, became the general manager and headed the company when it grew into a virtual money machine. He helped Manfred become one of the richest men in town.

"I am tired, Manfred. The years I have left, I want to live in Spain with my wife." Richard had married Consuelo who came to Schlutup with her parents during the first boom years of the German post war economy. Rumors that she was extraordinarily beautiful had been the talk of the town in the earlier years; she was seldom seen in public.

"Richard, I knew you were married, but I never met your wife. Are you sure she wants to return to Spain? Are you sure you want to live there?"

"She wants to go back. We have been there twice together. I think I'd like it."

Bürgermeister Borge invited Schlutup's business leaders and personalities to the customary New Year's Eve gathering at the *Ratskeller* in City Hall. Former mayors Scholte and Wendt were there, Judge Moltke, Sam Morgenstern, school principals, Kurt Lansen, his wife Ilse, and Richard Groth with Consuelo whose exotic beauty, now in her late sixties, was still evident.

Ferdinand Borge took Manfred aside. "Can we talk? This is in confidence, you see. I will not seek another term. I would approach ninety before my six years are up. Now, I hear Groth is retiring. I guess that will get you involved in the business again, right?"

"What are you getting at?"

"Wouldn't you want to try again? I can't think of a better man. I have less than two years left, time for you to make your intentions known."

"Hold it a minute there, Herr Bürgermeister! Look, Ferdinand, I have no such intentions."

"Not so loud, Manfred. What I mean is, your son will take over the business in a year or two and you are free to dedicate your talents to the city again."

"No, no. But let me tell you something…"

Richard Groth and his wife approached them where they were standing, Champagne glasses in hand. "Are we interrupting? We want to get going. We leave early tomorrow morning."

Consuelo added, "I enjoyed living in your town for fifty years, now is time to return to my country."

"It was our pleasure to have you," said the mayor. "Please, keep in touch and return often!"

"Richard, Frau Groth, sorry to see you leave. It's been almost a lifetime."

"Come and visit us," said Consuelo. "Adios!"

They walked away and Manfred said, "what a lovely woman. Never got to know her."

"Yes, yes. Now, where were we? You were saying?"

Manfred thought for a moment. "I'll talk to you in a couple of days. I might have an idea, just an idea, you see." Then they rejoined the party that began to break up.

"Frieda, I have to find someone to take Richard's place; someone on the board…"

"Let Manfred come back from Berlin. He's ready to take over."

"No. He will be the next mayor."

***

Schlutup enjoyed a few days of false spring, usually followed by another onslaught of winter before its final surrender. Pigeons scurried about on Manfred Scholte Platz, searching for scraps of food between the cobblestones. The proprietor of the café had set out a couple of tables covered with white tablecloths, which he secured with clamps against sudden gusts of wind.

Ilse Lansen and Frieda Scholte often met at the café on Fridays. They sat at a table inside, not trusting the weather on this afternoon in early March.

"I am worried about Kurt," Ilse confided in Frieda. "He is often so distant. Sometimes, it seems he wants to tell me something, and then he backs off."

"He went through a lot, Ilse. He almost died. It's to be expected. I think he has come a long way. His hair turned white, but it really looks good on him."

"Yes, Frieda, but that's not it. Even before that, something was bothering him."

"You never asked?"

"We've always given each other space, never pry into each other. We have a good marriage, are open about everything, except... I don't know."

"I remember one day on our terrace last summer. Manfred asked him, 'What's the matter? Why are you so quiet?' Remember that?"

"No. When? What did he say?"

"He just shook his head and said, 'I'm okay.' I didn't think much about it then."

"You see? That happens more often lately." Ilse took a sip of her *Campari*. "He falls silent and broods. I wish he would tell me, but it has to come from him."

Frieda signaled the waiter for another espresso." Look, Ilse, if you are so worried, let Manfred try. You see, they are very close. Sometimes with a friend it's easier."

"I don't know. It's like a deep-rooted guilt. Once I asked him if he didn't want to go and see Breslau again. It's now Wroclaw, in Poland. He grew up there." Ilse leaned across the small round table, closer to Frieda. Her voice trembled as she continued. "'No, never,' he said vehemently. 'I can never go back there.' I am afraid something happened to him when he was young."

"Let Manfred talk to him," Frieda repeated. "Manfred, in his own way, is good at that. But only if you agree."

"Thanks. Let me think about it. And thanks for listening to me. This is something that's always on my mind."

The shadows of the bare trees on the opposite side of the plaza grew long and the clock in the *Rathaus* tower struck five. "What, five o'clock? He will wonder where I am." Frieda searched her bag for some bills to pay for her coffee and Ilse's *Campari*. "It's on me today. You pay next time. Let me run. I'll call you."

That evening, Frieda asked Manfred if he had noticed something odd about Kurt. "Ilse said something to me today."

"About Kurt? I don't know. I think he's doing rather well. Get's tired, but think, he almost got killed four, five years ago."

"No, she says it's not that. Goes back to his youth. When he grew up in Breslau. Like something happened to him there."

"Why doesn't she ask him?"

"She can't. He won't talk about it. Would you... You are good friends, maybe he would tell you."

"Frieda, it's between them. We can't get involved. They have to work out their own problems."

"But we should help them, if we can."

***

Mayor Ferdinand Borge had approached Manfred at the New Year's Eve gathering. "I can't think of a better man than you to run this city again after I retire," he told him.

A couple of months later, he called Manfred. "Have you thought about it? It's time you begin your campaign. You have my backing, but you must make your intentions known before I can endorse you."

Manfred Scholte met with the aging mayor in his office at City Hall. "Ferdinand, I thank you for your confidence, but it's out of the question. I have a different plan."

Borge wanted to interrupt; however, Manfred stopped him. "Hear me out, please."

The mayor made a gesture indicating his impatience, but he said, "Go ahead."

"I found the solution. Listen to this, Ferdinand. The name Scholte will be on the ballot, only it will be my son."

"Manfred Junior? But, he is too young."

"He will be my age, when I first became mayor—almost, anyway. In a year, Manfred Junior will have his law degree from Humboldt. Ferdinand, my son will become the first mayor of Schlutup with a degree in law. Yes, you heard me right: he will become the next mayor."

"No, no, no. Why? And what will you do?"

"Since Richard Groth retired and moved to Spain, I am again head-ing the corporation, at least part-time. Frieda bugs me to give it up, so I reached an agreement with Sam Morgenstern. His son, David, will take over the Scholte concern as the new CEO. He specializes in corporate law and has assisted me with legal questions in the past. He knows my operation." Leaning back in his chair, Manfred added, "I will finally be able to retire."

Manfred Scholte Junior, just thirty-five years old, began campaign-ing for mayor of Schlutup while still attending law school in Ber-lin. Shuttling between the capital and his hometown, he organized a team of strategists and volunteers never before seen in this city. In an open-air speech on Manfred Scholte Platz, he proclaimed his candidacy with the slogan: *Scholte—the name that will carry you into the twenty-first century!*

Ferdinand Borge reluctantly agreed to Manfred's proposal. With the backing of the incumbent mayor—and Scholte money— the campaign took off to a good start. The young man had charm and charisma. Women would almost certainly vote for him. His closest competitor, Judge Moltke, was his only real rival. A labor union official and the city manager, the two other candidates, both had little support.

Frieda, too, was happy with the prospect of having Junior in City Hall. "It's our town, Manfred. Don't you feel like it's our town? I think it should be renamed *Scholtestadt*. How does that sound to you, huh? *Scholtestadt*... better than Schlutup. What does it mean, anyway?"

"Comes from the old *Plattdeutsch*, means to close. *Schluten*. Has to do with the time when they closed the gates at night. *Schlut up* means unlock, in the mornings, to let the trades people in. Open trade. Welcome. Prosperity—all that. They're not gonna change that."

"I was just thinking..."

"Yeah, you always think too much."

"Well, something else I was thinking... Ilse said to me it would be all right if you had a little talk with Kurt. You know... What I was telling you. Would you?"

"What about? Can't they work it out, whatever it is? Look, I hate to meddle in other people's affairs."

"Manfred, this is something that might be hard for them to confront. She thinks there is some dark secret tied up in him. Be a good friend and help him loosen that knot."

"Okay. Are they coming over? Do I have to go over there? How am I gonna do it? How am I gonna start? Who knows what I'll run into."

"Just give it a try. I will meet Ilse tomorrow for lunch and some shopping. Drop in on him, as you sometimes do."

Manfred still felt uncomfortable about it, but the following day he called Kurt. "What are you doing? Mind if I come over for a beer? Frieda is out shopping, so... Okay?"

Summer was a little late in 1996. June was like April, with showers and strong gusts coming over the Baltic. Kurt had turned on the radiator to get the chill out of the room.

Manfred wore only a jacket. "The sun came out for a moment. I thought I didn't need a coat. Oh, you have the heat on. Feels good."

"I made a pot of tea. Pour some rum into it. Better than beer in this weather."

They sat down and continued with small talk about the weather; the politics of Helmut Kohl and if Gerhard Schröder would become chancellor; Bill Clinton and the German-US relations and so on.

Manfred went back to their days in the garden shack. "You came from Breslau, huh? Where were you during the war? You weren't in the Wehrmacht?"

"No, I was... I was, I was still in school. Later I went with my mother... We spent time in... We moved a lot. My father... He was dead." Kurt reached for the pot. "More tea?"

"Yeah, thanks. So, what happened? Your father died young, then. How old were you when he died?"

"Ah, sixteen." Kurt poured the tea. "Help yourself to the rum. I don't know how much you like. You are from Neuendorf, right? Not far from here. You told me your father wasn't a locksmith, but what did he do?"

"He had a bicycle shop. Sewing machines, vacuum cleaners, stuff like that." Manfred dropped two lumps of sugar into his tea and added a good measure of rum.

"I'm not supposed to drink too much alcohol," said Kurt. "Not good with my medication." A strand of silvery hair fell over his forehead. He pushed it back with his familiar gesture. "Well, I don't drink much anyway."

"What are you taking?"

"Stuff for my heart, the blood flow through the lungs, to take the pressure off my chest..."

"Well, then go easy on the rum."

"Ah, what the hell. I don't really care."

"Kurt, what is it that bothers you? I noticed for some time there is something on your mind, something you don't want to talk about."

"Right. Something I don't want to talk about. So, let's leave it as that."

"No, Kurt. It's eating you up inside. You're unhappy and..."

"Who told you I am unhappy? Ilse? Look, we have a good marriage—better than most. We all carry something around with us."

"If I had a problem, I would come to you, my best friend. You said your father had died when you were sixteen. Was that in the war? Was he in the army? Did he get shot?"

Kurt became agitated. He trembled and his voice broke. "Yes. He got shot."

"Where? In Poland? In '39? What happened to you and your mother? Where did..."

"All right. He was dead." There were tears in Kurt's eyes. "My mother and I moved. Dammit, I don't want to talk about it." He spilled some tea as he lifted the cup to his lips. "Don't..."

Manfred was moved. He felt Kurt was close to revealing something to him. "Kurt, listen to me. I am your friend. Whatever it is you're telling me, I'll keep it secret, if you want me to. But please, get it off your chest. Please."

Kurt stood up, walked toward the window. Leaves were twirling on their branches in the wind gusts, scrambling about like the thoughts in his tortured mind. He stood with his hands in his pockets and stared through the glass, through the trees, into the distance. Softly, as if to himself, he said, "I shot him."

Manfred sat silently.

"I shot the bastard," Kurt said through clenched teeth. He pounded the glass with his fist and screamed, "I shot the bastard." The window shattered, a thin stream of blood trickled from Kurt's fist. Wind entering through the broken glass ruffled his hair.

After a long, silent moment, Manfred got up. He slowly walked over to Kurt, stood behind him and softly put one hand on his friend's shoulder. With his other hand he removed a handkerchief from his pocket and gently, carefully wrapped it around Kurt's bloody wrist.

Ilse Lansen and Frieda Scholte lingered in front of the café. "I think he wants to talk, Frieda. He made attempts. I wish I knew what troubles him. Then I could help him."

"Maybe he and Manfred had a good talk. Go, Ilse. Want me to come with you?"

"No, thanks. See you tomorrow."

Ilse walked briskly, holding her coat together at the neck against a cold breeze. In front of her apartment building she stepped on broken glass, but paid no attention.

Manfred greeted her at the door with not more than a nod. Kurt sat on the couch, his hair disheveled, a handkerchief around his right hand. He did not look up.

She did not yet know what happened as she hung up her coat. Then she noticed the broken window, a wave of cold air coming from it.

"I was just leaving," Manfred said softly. "He needs you now."

"Thanks." Ilse hesitated. "Can you stay, for a moment?"

"You don't need me. It's best... just you two. Me and Frieda... We'll call you." Quietly he left, closing the door soundlessly.

Ilse sat next to her husband, put one hand on his knee, leaning her shoulder against his.

"I killed him. Shot him with his own gun. He couldn't touch me anymore, couldn't hit my mother. Shot him in the chest at arm's length." Kurt sat motionless and talked in a monotone, his injured hand in his lap.

Ilse did not respond, but took his bloody hand in hers. They sat without words for a long time; then Kurt let his head slowly fall on her shoulder.

The following morning a repairman showed up. "You have a broken window? I'll fix it. Takes me less than half an hour."

Kurt stayed in bed, recovering as if from a long ailment.

***

During the week that followed, Kurt remained silent about the issue. Ilse knew he had stepped over a threshold, bared his conscience. He was incommunicative, avoided intimacy, shied away from all conversation that might lead to the subject of his tragic youth.

Ilse did not pursue the matter for several days. She was especially gentle with him. Patience, she told herself; lifting his long kept secret must have changed his entire being; he needs time to adjust.

Besides Ilse, only Manfred and Frieda had knowledge of what Kurt had revealed, but they still did not know what led him to reach for the gun and shoot his father.

Manfred discussed it with Frieda. "It must have been an act of desperation, perhaps of self-defense, to kill his own father. What else could have driven him to such an action, such irreversible deed, such a desperate solution?" The overwhelming story of Kurt's deep secret brought Manfred back to his habit of using fancy speech. "All these years he must have lived under a cloud of fear and guilt."

"You relieved him of a burden he could no longer carry, dear," Frieda commended him. "I met Ilse today. She is so grateful to you. Kurt still doesn't want to talk about it. She says, it will take time and she's not pushing him."

"He unburdened only half of the story."

"Ilse said she already knew a little more, but she didn't tell me what it was."

Ilse understood Kurt. They had been married for more than thirty-five years. They were always direct, straightforward with each other, but in this instance only a slow, careful approach might lead him to open the door to his innermost conscience.

They sat comfortably together on an evening watching television, as was their custom. After the news, a documentary on families living in abusive and violent circumstances came on. *"Adult subject matter, not recommended for viewing by..."* Kurt clicked the remote and switched to another program.

"Can't we watch that? Kurt, we have always been open with each other." Ilse decided not to circumvent the subject, but come directly to the point. She took the remote from his hand and turned the television off. "Won't you tell me what made you pick up that gun and shoot your father?"

He stared in front of him, unmoved. Then he slowly raised his shoulders and let them drop.

"You are a gentle, good man. There is no malice in you toward anybody. You even forgave Wolfgang who tried to kill you."

"I didn't forgive *him*." Kurt spoke in a low voice. "I forgave myself. I was Wolfgang."

After a pause he went on. "I was my father. I felt the bullet entering my chest."

Ilse was silent. Then slowly, calmly she asked, "Do you think you deserved to die?"

"No. Not any more. I forgave myself."

Ilse had reached deep into his psyche and found that there was much more than she had expected. *It's enough for now,* she thought. *It is still too hard for him.* "I love you, Kurt."

They did not often express their feelings; there was no need for them to say what they both knew.

"You know, my father was a musician with the *Staatskapelle* in Breslau. Played the flugelhorn." Kurt surprised Ilse with this sudden disclosure.

Sitting in the casino garden in Neustrand, they listened to the light operatic melodies played by an ensemble consisting of piano, violin and cello. They took advantage of the first warm day that year, enjoying a piece of pastry and coffee in this seaside resort.

Ilse had not pried into his past since their last talk on the subject, several days earlier.

"That must have been before the war. You were very young then."

"The Nazis threw him out in '36 because he had a Polish name. Lanski. Ludwig Lanski."

"What did he do after they threw him out?"

"Nothing. He drank. Then he forced me... He hit my mother. I was thirteen."

"He wasn't in the war?"

"No. He had to work in a factory. You want another cup of coffee?"

"Yes." Ilse signaled the waiter. "He hit your mother? And what did he do to you? You said he forced you... To do what, Kurt?"

The waiter brought their coffee and removed the empty cups. Kurt hesitated. He looked over the dunes and the beach out to the ocean. The soft breeze ruffled his hair.

"Ugly things. Disgusting things. He beat my mother and made her watch."

"He did that when you were thirteen?"

"No, he did that long before. Since I was much younger. But it got worse when he no longer played in the orchestra."

Ilse thought he had said enough and did not want him to overdo it. He still had to make an effort with every breath he took. "Don't exert yourself, Kurt. Relax for a moment. See the seagulls? How they glide so gracefully just above the waves."

"When the Nazis rounded up all the Jews and expelled the Poles, he went into hiding. One night he came back and forced me to go with him. He sent me to school and picked me up every day. Disguised himself as an old man. I didn't see my mother for weeks."

"Take it easy, Kurt. You don't have to go on if you…"

"He made me touch him and he touched me and I had to… had to…" Kurt brushed his hair back and passed the back of his hand over his eyes. "I took his pistol from his coat pocket. I didn't know if it was loaded, but I hoped so."

"I understand. You had no choice. You had to do it. It was not wrong, what you did."

Kurt could not hold the cup in his trembling hand. Coffee spilled over the tablecloth and his shirt. Ilse took the cup from him.

"I saw the black hole in the middle of his naked chest. Then blood ran down from it to his navel. He sank to the floor."

"Shhh, shhh. Easy, Kurt. Easy, easy. Calm yourself. I am right here with you. I am right here. Let's sit for a moment. Let's wait."

The sun sank behind the wooded elevation in the west and the light breeze turned cooler. The waiter came to remove the dishes and to exchange the stained tablecloth for a fresh one. Ilse asked for the check.

After some fifteen minutes they walked back to the bus stop for the ride home.

***

Summer faded into fall, and winter was not far off. While the enormous event in Kurt and Ilse's lives unfolded, the citizens of Schlutup followed their every-day routines. Unemployment had dropped further. The shipyard held its own with new orders for repairs and maintenance of coastal vessels, and the fish packing plant expanded operations. The food distribution center added truck drivers and cargo handlers, as the town continued to grow. Still, the city budget was in the red.

Manfred Junior, confident to defeat his rival Judge Moltke and to become the next mayor, conferred with Ferdinand Borge. Together they devised a plan to balance the budget during the first year of the new administration.

The trick was the promise of *No New Taxes* on income, property and services. Increased taxes on utility companies, however, would result in higher monthly bills for the consumer. Such hidden taxes and similar deceiving stratagems, employed by administrations around the world, were designed to ensure Manfred Scholte's success as the youngest mayor the city ever had.

Manfred Scholte Junior and the incumbent Mayor Ferdinand Borge met in private at the older man's residence adjacent to City Hall. Over a glass of sherry the mayor lectured Manfred, "'You can fool all the people some of the time…' You know that? 'You can fool some of the people all the time…' Know who said that?"

"Yes, Herr Borge," answered Manfred, "'…but you can't fool all the people all the time'. Abraham Lincoln, US president said that in 1864. And, yes, I also know that it is still true."

"A wise man, that Lincoln. A very wise man." Borge flicked the ash from his cigar. "He was a lawyer. You will be a lawyer. I hope you will have a lot more than that in common with Mister Lincoln." He paused. "Now, there is one thing. You were involved in a scandal back in '92, '93. Some people will still remember that."

"Some of the people, Herr Borge, but not all the people," Manfred laughed. He stood up. "I already took too much of your time. Tomorrow morning I'll drive back to Berlin. I have been accelerating my studies and will take my exam at the end of next semester."

"You are a diligent young man. I never had more than a few years of high school, like your father." Then he added, "Fritz Wendt was a clever mayor, but he overestimated his own powers. In the end his luck ran out. Be prudent, young man, be prudent."

After three semesters of basic studies, Manfred Junior scrambled through the five grueling mandatory semesters to become a *Volljurist*, a full-fledged lawyer. In the summer of 1997, he passed the *Staatsexamen* in jurisprudence.

While attending law school in Berlin, he made the acquaintance of an exceptionally bright and attractive young woman who also studied at Humboldt University to become a lawyer. Originally from Kiev, Ukraine, Olga Lidovskaya was fluent in Russian, Polish, English and German. After dating for several weeks, Manfred learned that Olga had spent a year and a half in Schlutup.

"That was in 1990 to '91. The mass movement swept me into

town when they opened the border," she explained.

He hesitated, puzzled and uncertain how to ask the next question. *I didn't exactly live a model life in those years, but...* "Were you familiar with the *Rote Katze*, the night club? I just thought I might have seen you... Not that I was a regular patron..."

"Are you asking me if I worked for Madam Gudrun? The answer is yes, but not at the *Rote Katze*. She had already moved to a better location. I wanted to go to university; what better way to make money in a hurry?" She looked at him teasingly. "You are shocked, right? You said you were from Schlutup. That's why I didn't tell you that I once lived there."

Manfred was not shocked . If anything, this made her more intriguing. He was in love and decided to marry her. He proposed the day they celebrated the completion of their long and exhausting studies at Humboldt. Olga was not sure if she wanted to return to Schlutup and become the mayor's wife. *Would I be remembered?* At Madam Gudrun's she had been the favorite of some of the more influential personas. *But that is seven years in the past.*

"I can get you in touch with Morgenstern and Sons, the best law firm in town. There is a position open. Corporate law. Interested?"

Olga was adventurous and a free spirit. "Get me that job, and we will talk marriage later, all right? I have to test the water, get my feet wet, see how it goes. If they remember me, they might want to run me out of town."

"Did you use your own name then?"

"No. Madam called me "her Black Madonna" after the painting in Krakow. Because of my black hair. So I was known as Madonna."

"In '93 Madam Gudrun bought my father's mansion. It became the Gentlemen's Club. There was a scandal a few years back. Drugs, illegal aliens. The Judge gave her a stiff penalty. Today she runs a very respectable establishment."

"Wow! You must know her well then. Is she still around? She must be quite old."

"Yeah, I guess about seventy, but I don't know her personally." Manfred returned to Schlutup, bringing Olga with him. She had several interviews with Sam Morgenstern who was impressed with her credentials and he hired her as an associate. She settled easily into the position vacated by his son David.

The end phase of the campaign was in full swing. Judge Moltke had fallen further behind in the polls and in October Manfred Scholte Junior was elected. Ferdinand Borge handed the reins over to his young successor and retired to his country home near Neustrand. Manfred moved into the Bürgermeister's residence.

Olga, still unsure about Manfred's proposal, rented a modest apartment. Two months into her new situation, she still had not been recognized or remembered. At the inauguration reception in the *Ratskeller*, she met the outgoing mayor, dignitaries of the town council, important members of the business community and Manfred's parents. Judge Moltke had conceded defeat, but did not make an appearance. Kurt and Ilse Lansen were among the guests. Krista was invited, but she declined. Since Karl's death she had remained close to her old friends, but rarely attended social gatherings.

Although Olga had not yet made a commitment, Manfred introduced her to his parents as his fiancée. She smiled gracefully.

She thought there were some familiar faces among the male guests, but she was not sure. None of the men gave an indication that they remembered her. She wore her hair cut short, pageboy style, and looked stunning in a fuchsia cocktail dress.

"How about it, Olga? Will you become the mayor's wife?" Manfred repeated his proposal later in the evening.

"Does it have to be right away?"

"I introduced you to my parents as my fiancée. Others heard it too."

"I'll think about it."

***

By the end of 1998 the economy of the city moved in the right direction and at fiscal closing in April the following year, the accounting department announced a balanced budget. In a public declaration Mayor Manfred Scholte Junior reiterated his campaign promise, *With Scholte into the Twenty-first Century.*

To most of the citizens, the balancing of the city budget was meaningless. The cost of living had increased dramatically and although City Hall trumpeted the great progress over previous administrations, the per-capita income did not keep up with the rising expenses for heating oil, electricity and the higher water bills. People complained, but as always, they adjusted, tightened their belts, got used to it.

Krista's pension was not eligible for a boost. "Your son, he don't care for the elderly," she reproached Manfred. "If this goes on, I'll still end up in the poor house of the *Heilsarmee.* I'd rather die." She was only half-serious; she took everything in stride; she was not a complainer.

"Krista, are you in trouble? You come to me if you need something," Frieda told her. "As we said, we look out for you."

"Yeah, thanks. I know. Listen, I haven't seen Ilse for a long time. Are they all right?" Krista had heard the whole story of Kurt's dilemma from Ilse after he had unburdened himself, first with Manfred and then with his wife. "You know, I've always felt there was something about Kurt, even in the early days in the garden. I have always known something wasn't right."

"Can you stay for a while? They're coming over."

"Oh good, I don't have nothin' to do, nowhere to go in hurry."

Kurt's health had steadily improved during the past year and a half. His breathing hardly gave him any trouble. He still walked with a cane, but that was more from habit than necessity. Approaching seventy-seven, with a full head of white hair and his natural tanned complexion, he had become a picture of health since he no lnger carried the weight of his horrible youth alone.

"Something I don't understand," Krista asked him as they were having coffee. "Your name was Lanski. When did you change it?"

Kurt was amused by her uncomplicated, blunt way to ask him so directly. He had overcome his reluctance to talk about his ordeal. "We moved around a lot, my mother and I. At first we never stayed more than a few days in one place. Neighbors had found the body the morning after... you know. When the war broke out, they forgot about the...the murder. My mother died in Dresden when I was eighteen. That's when I changed my name."

"You weren't in the Wehrmacht. How so?" Manfred was curious.

"There was no record of me. I had disappeared; I no longer existed. All through the war I lived in hiding. I was afraid to register for military service. They would have discovered that I was a murderer."

"Stop it, Kurt," Ilse reprimanded him. "You are not a murderer. You did what you had to do. That's not murder."

"It's all right, Ilse. I know. I don't feel guilty anymore." He thought for a moment. "I was just thinking: that was sixty years ago. Don't remember the exact date, but I still feel how I pulled the trigger. It was harder than I thought, needed a lot of pressure. Then the recoil... I hoped he was dead."

They were quiet around the table. At last Krista broke the silence. "Well, he was, right? You ran home to your mother, took the pistol with you, right? And then you found out for sure next morning, right?"

"Krista!" Frieda admonished her.

"It's okay. You know the rest. I met Kurzer. He brought me to the garden house."

"More coffee?" Frieda asked.

"I want a drink. You, Kurt? I don't have any *Wacholder*, but this twelve-year old scotch will do. Ladies? A liqueur?"

"Save it for New Year's," said Frieda. "We'll celebrate all together, right? Let's invite Klaus and Helga, and Hans-Peter with his two Ninas, too."

***

A messenger delivered a sealed envelope marked 'personal' to Olga Lidovskaya at her desk at Morgenstern & Sons. A feeling of foreboding mixed with curiosity overcame her. She broke the seal and extracted a hand-written note. *Madonna – it would be my pleasure to have your company in the afternoon of Thursday next. Affectionately, Gudrun.*

Olga replaced the card in it's envelope and stashed it in her briefcase. She had difficulty concentrating on the project Sam

Morgenstern had entrusted to her. *How did she find out that I am here? Who has recognized me and informed Madam Gudrun?* She decided not to tell Manfred about it, at least not yet. Years of legal studies had honed her mind in logical thinking. She evaluated her options, from ignoring the note or declining the invitation, to accepting and confronting the consequences.

By evening she concluded that she had to accept the invitation. Not to respond, or to decline, even gracefully, could have results beyond her control. *I hate clichés, but what the hell: Take the bull by the horn. Roll with the punches. You made your bed, now lie in it. No pain, no gain. Calm before the storm—no, not that one.*

Before she left the office on Thursday afternoon, she put a call through to Manfred and left a message on his private line. *Hi, I am visiting an old acquaintance who has invited me. See you tonight.* She was sure he would know whom she meant by old acquaintance.

"I am delighted to see you, Madonna. Here, in the privacy of my boudoir we can talk intimately. Nobody will hear us." Reclining on her super-sized bed, Gudrun reached for a button by her side. "Coffee, tea or something stronger, my dear? Sit here, close to me." She pointed to a comfortable armchair.

Olga was appalled by the enormity of her former employer, but tried not to let her consternation show. *Must weigh at least five times my own weight.* "Good to see you, too, Madam. May I ask how you learned that I had returned to Schlutup? Who did…"

"Oh, Madonna, this is still a small town, even though it has grown. Let me just say, we have common acquaintances."

A knock at the door interrupted them. "Come in," and to Olga, "what would you like, dear?" To her butler she said, "my tea, please, Bruno."

"Just a glass of water, if I may."

Bruno left quietly and Gudrun resumed. "Where were we? Ah, I have known for some time of your liaison with Herr Manfred Scholte, your fiancé, and that you are working with Herr Morgenstern, a close friend of mine. He is quite pleased with you, by the way."

"Sam Morgenstern, my boss? He knows...? Was it he who informed you?"

Madam Gudrun shifted her bulk under the light blanket to receive her tea from the butler who had silently entered the room. He moved a small table next to Olga, placed a glass of water on it and withdrew.

"Now, now, Madonna. I cannot tell you who informed me. You know that would be wrong." She smiled sincerely. "My establishment prides itself of its discretion."

"What discretion? If everybody seems to know? And, please, do not call me Madonna. My name is Olga Lidovskaya. I am not the same person."

"Oh, dear, I did not mean to upset you."

"How do you know so much about me? I hoped my past would remain undiscovered. It's been eight years... Have I changed so little?"

"You are as beautiful as you were then, Madonna. Do not be alarmed, but I give you a warning as your friend. You know how fond I have always been of you." Gudrun stirred some artificial sweetner into her tea. "Only a few of my guests know that you have returned... Judge Moltke among them. There is a longstanding feud between him and the Scholtes." She accommodated her massive body into a more comfortable position. "Judge Moltke holds a grudge against them ever since he had failed to send young Manfred to prison in a sex and drug case some seven years ago. Losing the election to him in 1997 added to his aversion against them."

"Judge Moltke... If he is a friend of yours..."

"Let me just say, the judge and I have an understanding, if you know what I mean. I would not term it a friendship."

Olga had learned enough. *A big scandal is looming, and I am the pawn.* "Thank you for your kindness, Madam. I'd better go now. Thank you... and good-bye."

Madam Gudrun pressed the button. "I am sorry, Madonna. The best of luck to you." The butler appeared and Olga left through the door he held open for her. *Judge Moltke...*

Olga returned to her office. The staff had already left. She sat at her desk for only a short moment before taking out her laptop computer. She typed, *Herr Samuel Morgenstern, circumstances oblige me to relinquish my post immediately. You will understand my decision without explanation. I have learned much during the nearly two years I had the privilege of working with you and I thank you for the confidence you had in me. With my apologies for my hasty departure, Olga Lidovskaya.*

Once more Manfred listened to the tape. *Visiting an old acquaintance...* He hit the erase button and leaned back in his leather chair. A second later he sat up straight and struck the top of his desk with his palm. *Damn, this had to happen. If the old whore knows, the whole town knows.*

He punched in Olga's home number. *Busy signal.* A minute later, still busy. It was long after office hours and City Hall was all but deserted. There were only a few cars still in the lot beside his BMW, parked in the space marked Bürgermeister.

Manfred drove to the building where Olga lived. Her Opel was not there. Sitting in his car, he called her *Handi* from the car phone. No answer. Walking up the single flight of stairs, Manfred already realized that she was gone. He had the key to her apartment, but did not need it. The door stood ajar. The buzzing of the unattended telephone was annoyingly shrill in the sparsely furnished room. He replaced the receiver in its cradle, opened a closet and found it empty. On the dresser was a hastily scribbled note. *You will understand. Do not try to find me. It is better for you and for me. Olga.*

Sam Morgenstern circulated a memo through his office, saying Fräulein Olga Lidovskaya had left the firm due to a family emergency. The local press picked it up and reported that Mayor Scholte, her fiancé, had no comment.

Frieda said to her husband, "I don't know, but I have the feeling there's more than he is telling us."

"Stop looking for clues. Always looking for clues. It's all gossip. He told me he knew for a long time that she had to go back to... wherever she came from."

"Kiev, dear, in the Ukraine. That's what he told you, but I don't believe it. It's a mother's intuition," she mumbled. "Family emergency... it's always a family emergency."

Olga Lidovskaya's hasty departure from Schlutup left a lot of people guessing, but her association with the Gentlemen's Club and the madam remained a secret within the walls of Madam Gudrun's mansion.

"I did what I deemed best to protect the integrity of my establishment. I warned Madonna and she took my warning seriously. She's gone." Madam Gudrun taunted the judge. "Isn't that what you wanted, Herr Moltke?"

"That's not what I wanted. I wanted to embarrass young Scholte and his family by exposing who she was."

"You can still do that. If you do, however, I would see to it that your preference for certain sexual excesses would become known. Your days on the bench would be over, your wife would leave you and you might even end up in jail." Gudrun revelled in having the judge in a corner. "I like the Scholtes better than you, Herr Moltke. You know that."

"I also know of your money schemes. I let you get away with it the last time. If revealed, you would certainly spend a long time behind bars."

"So we both have a weapon, like in the cold war. It all depends on who blinks first." She quipped, "You be the judge, Herr Moltke."

***

Frieda made the effort to call her daughter in Paris. "Birgit, your father booked the ballroom at the *Hotel Zum Anker* for the millennium celebration. Won't you come and be with us? Bring a friend or whoever you like. It would mean so much to me."

"There are celebrations here too, mother. I will think about it. I'll let you know."

Her rather cool response left Frieda with the same empty feeling as always after calling her, and she did not call her often.

"I told you to leave her alone," grumbled her husband. "She doesn't need us. She doesn't want us. Leave her alone."

Frieda consoled herself. "Manfred will join us after the reception at City Hall."

They invited government officials, dignitaries, businessmen and -women, merchants from their community, Kurt and Ilse and, of course, their old friends Klaus and Hans-Peter with their families.

"And, Manfred, we could ask Richard Groth and Consuelo to come. Wouldn't it be nice if they could come?"

"You can suggest it. They might not want to leave sunny Spain to freeze their butts off in the frigid north."

Klaus Lietke sent a note. "We will definitely be there", and Hans-Peter telephoned enthusiastically, "Sure! We don't want to miss it. Ninotchka says hello." Frieda heard her in the background: "Dajosh, Schlutup!" —whatever that means.

Nina Hauser, eleven years old, was a smart and lively child. She was popular among her peers, maintained good grades in school, and was mature for her age.

"I think she is old enough to learn her origin; that she was adopted; that her parents had died," Hans-Peter suggested. "I think you should tell her, mother to daughter."

Ninotchka agreed and the evening before their trip to Schlutup for the big New Year's celebration, she sat down with her daughter for a "serious talk".

"Nina, you remember car crash I told you about?" she began. "You were in that crash, Nina. You were not hurt, but your... the people in front seat were killed."

"The car crash? Yes, I know. But why was I in that car? Who were those people?"

"Nina, your Papa took you out from burning car, but the... the others, they were both dead. Nina—they were your parents."

"They were? You and Papa are... You are not my parents? But I love you. And you love me, right?" Nina hugged her mother. "You are my Mama. And my other parents, I mean the dead ones, they died in the burning car?"

"No, Nina, they died in crash. Already dead before explosion and fire."

After a moment Nina asked, "How old was I? A baby?"

"Yes Nina, a baby. Only eighteen months. We are so lucky to have you."

"I am lucky, too. Papa saved me. Was it such a big crash?"

"It was big crash. Many car, many people hurt."

Nina let go of her mother. Not quite certain what to say, she asked, "Mama, what were their names? Did you know them? Do you know their names?"

"They were Frans and Mirna Trzebiez. We did not know them, but we found out they were from here, Katowice. So we move here."

"Then I am a real Polish girl, like you! But Papa, you are German."

Hans-Peter had joined them. "I am German, but I like it here in Poland. And Nina, nothing changes, you are our daughter and we love you. You are Nina Hauser."

"Papa, can't my name be Trzebiez? Nina Trzebiez. I love you, but can I have my real name? No? How about Nina Trzebiez Hauser?"

"You can change your name when you're eighteen," her father allowed.

"Sixteen. She can change sixteen," Ninotchka interfered. "For now is Hauser. Maybe middle name Trzebiez. In school still is Hauser."

"I love you, Papa." She hugged him. She gave her mother a kiss and went to her room.

Nina Trzebiez. I like it. Trzebiez Hauser. Frans and Mirna—I wonder what they were like. She fell asleep.

"Hanse-Pet, you think we did right thing, tell her truth about who she is?"

"I think so. You did very well, the way you told her."

"She is *wunderbar.* And you are good father."

"You are good mamuchka."

In the morning, long before the sun came up, they were on their way to Schlutup.

***

Manfred knew who his enemy was: Judge Moltke. The words of the old Mayor Ferdinand Borge flashed through his mind: *Be prudent.*

He did not attempt to find Olga. He had lately been seen in restaurants around town with his personal secretary, and rumors had it that they were romantically involved.

The reception at City Hall ended in late afternoon. The young mayor was popular among his staff and it had been a boisterous party.

Manfred, his secretary and some of his coworkers rode in the chauffeur-driven limousine to the *Hotel Zum Anker* to join the festivities already in progress in the ballroom.

At the same time a social gathering was underway in the Gentlemen's Club. It was one of the rare occasions on which the madam came down from her private apartment to greet her guests. The small, select group of her patrons included former mayor Fritz Wendt, an industrialist from the Rhineland, two executives of the former *Hansawerke*, an Airbus engineer and her "cold war opponent" Judge Moltke. Sam Morgenstern made a brief appearance before heading for the *Hotel Zum Anker*.

The new millennium was one hour away. Fireworks, staged on a barge, were to begin at the stroke of midnight. Thousands moved toward the harbor, bundled up and braced against the icy wind that came across the water.

The city had erected a viewing platform for the mayor, his immediate staff and guests. Manfred and his secretary took their place on a raised dais in the center. A fashionable brunette joined them: Birgit Scholte. Next to her stood a tall stranger. Manfred and Frieda, Kurt and Ilse, and Hans-Peter with Ninotchka and their daughter Nina huddled together for warmth. Not far from them Klaus Lietke and Richard Groth with their wives found room on the crowded stage.

The multitude began to count down the last seconds of the old year, drowning out the twelve strokes from the distant tower of city hall. The fireworks began with German punctuality, lighting the black sky with red and gold bursts, suggestive of the colors of the German national flag.

The elaborate spectacle lasted for nearly an hour, ending in a crescendo of color, light and noise reminiscent of heavy guns. The city remained alive through much of the night with sporadic firecrackers. The Scholtes retired with their friends to their home where they continued the celebration in private.

"Birgit!" Her mother at last had the opportunity to talk to her daughter. "I am so happy you came. You look good, haven't changed at all since we last saw you in Paris in '93."

"Ya, okay, Mother. Oh, this is Rose, my lover. We're together for the last six months."

"Enchantée, Madame," said the tall, rather masculine 'lover' Rose.

"Mhm." Frieda struggled to keep her composure. "Enchanted, too."

"Mother, we have to leave. Early flight from Hamburg in the morning. Say good-bye to father for me." She and Rose walked over to her brother, talked for a moment, and then they left.

Frieda was in tears. "Manfred, you wouldn't even talk to her," she complained to her husband. "Couldn't you at least say one word to her? Was that so hard for you? She is our daughter."

"Her lover? She said 'her lover'? And you want me to talk to them?" He shrugged. "What would you want me to say to them, huh? 'Pleased to meet you,' huh? Has she no decency?"

Kurt came over to them. "Don't be so hard on yourself, Manfred. Don't take it so hard."

"Yeah, Dad, you could have shown her that you cared. She is my sister, you know. By the way, this is my secretary, Fräulein Müller."

"Pleased to meet you," said his father and turned to refill his glass with champagne. "Kids, nothing but trouble," he grumbled. He spotted Hans-Peter talking with Richard and Klaus. Putting his arm on Klaus' shoulder he said, "The city put on a pretty good show, wouldn't you say so?" and to Richard, "it's great you and Consuelo came. Happy New Year!"

"Same to you, Manfred. Good to be here."

"I am glad we made the trip," Consuelo added.

"Manfred, did you meet my daughter? This is Nina," Hans-Peter proudly introduced her. "You saw her when she was two."

"I am Nina Trzebiez, Herr Scholte. Pleased to meet you," said the girl with grown-up flair and in perfect German.

Ninotchka shouted from across the room. "Still Hauser, Nina! Still Hauser until sixteen!"

Manfred explained, "We thought she should know. No secrets in my family."

The party broke up in the early morning on the first day of the twenty-first century.

Nobody was aware that shortly before midnight an ambulance had been summoned to Madam Gudrun's residence.

EPILOGUE

Olga Lidovskaya, after her precipitous flight from Schlutup six weeks earlier, settled in the tumultuous metropolis of Frankfurt. *If Manfred should try to find me, this would be the last place for him to look.* She moved in with a friend from law school and found temporary employment with a dubious, third-class firm thriving on frivolous law suits. She later formed her own firm, Lidovskaya, Attorney at Law.

Keeping her eyes open for news from Schlutup, and browsing the internet she found on the first day of January, 2000 a short news item: *Judge dead of heart attack in night club in the northern city of Schlutup.*

Madam Gudrun died that year of organ failure related to her obesity.

Manfred Scholte Junior was reelected in 2003 for a second term as mayor of Schlutup. He maintained a relationship with his secretary, but never married.

His parents continued a peaceful life, although they never reconciled with their estranged lesbian daughter. Birgit Scholte, successful couturier in Paris, did not return to Germany, except for annual fashion shows in Berlin.

Ilse Lansen survived Kurt who died at age eighty. His last years had been his happiest, free from the burden of guilt over the murder of his father.

Krista, Karl Berger's lifelong companion, who had been too frail to attend the New Year's festivities with her old friends, died in the spring of 2000.

Klaus and Helga Lietke enjoyed their family life into old age, with grandchildren and great-grandchildren.

Hans-Peter Hauser, the lighthearted, inconsiderate prankster of his youth, became the most thoughtful and loving father to his adopted daughter Nina. He and his vivacious wife Ninotchka moved to Warsaw when Nina entered university there. Throughout his long life he kept his youthfulness, by the side of Ninotchka.

CPSIA information can be obtained at www.ICGtesting.com
Printed in the USA
LVOW08s1246160116

470178LV00004B/149/P